Lady of the Lookout

As the Founder/CEO of NAVH, the only national health agency solely devoted to those who, although not totally blind, have an eye disease which could lead to serious visual impairment, I am pleased to recognize Thorndike Press* as one of the leading publishers in the large print field.

Founded in 1954 in San Francisco to prepare large print textbooks for partially seeing children, NAVH became the pioneer and standard setting agency in the preparation of large type.

Today, those publishers who meet our standards carry the prestigious "Seal of Approval" indicating high quality large print. We are delighted that Thorndike Press is one of the publishers whose titles meet these standards. We are also pleased to recognize the significant contribution Thorndike Press is making in this important and growing field.

Lorraine H. Marchi, L.H.D.
Founder/CEO
NAVH

* Thorndike Press encompasses the following imprints: Thorndike, Wheeler, Walker and Large Print Press.

Lady of the
Lookout

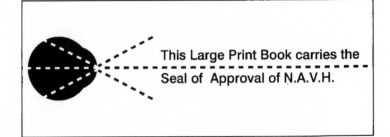

Lady of the Lookout

Colleen L. Reece
and
Albert B. Towne

Thorndike Press • Waterville, Maine

20032336

Published in 2004 by arrangement with Colleen L. Reece.

Thorndike Press® Large Print Candlelight.

The tree indicium is a trademark of Thorndike Press.

The text of this Large Print edition is unabridged.
Other aspects of the book may vary from the original edition.

Set in 16 pt. Plantin by Al Chase.

Printed in the United States on permanent paper.

ISBN 0-7862-7157-4 (lg. print : hc : alk. paper)

Preface

Albert B. Towne, my mother's brother, lived the rugged life described in this book. Raised in a western Washington logging town much like the fictional setting of Three Rivers, he climbed from valley to peak and saw with his own eyes the crows'-nests (lookout towers) where intrepid firewatchers served.

For two years I worked with "Uncle Curly," sharing his joy at reliving his own boyhood and teen years as he created accurate settings, believable characters, and an intriguing plot. We laughed and cried together; we talked often of God, His creation, and the gift of His Son. Albert's poem, "God's Country," which appears in chapter six, expresses his appreciation.

After Albert's death, his beloved wife Edith graciously consented to my revising the story to meet the needs of Heartsong Presents. I am proud and grateful as coauthor of *Lady of the Lookout* to offer a glimpse of a different world, a world that exists only in precious memories, and in the faith handed down by our forebears.

COLLEEN L. REECE

Prologue

Welcome to Three Rivers, Washington, a small lumber community snuggled in the heart of the vast timber region of the North-west. Like other small towns of the early twentieth century, Three Rivers boasts a population of about 300, depending on what old crony you ask. Yet Three Rivers is special. Miles away from civilization, families depend on each other in a unique way that generates a warm, friendly feeling far different from less isolated villages.

The hamlet took its name from the three rivers that run nearby: the Sauk, the Suiattle, and the Stilliguamish. Tame in summer, they run wild and free in flood season, inspiring awe in the most stouthearted Indian and white alike. "Town's like the bottom of a coffee mug," an old timer once told a curious "flatland furriner," local jargon for a visitor or new-comer. "You look up to the rim." Indeed, the fir and cedar-covered ridges that circle the town cause the eye to continue upward to the jagged but majestic white peaks that serrate the sky. "Most folks think we're real high here. 'Tain't so. We're about 600 feet elevation's all. That's why those mile-high mountains look so tall, and so close," he cackled.

"A true alpine village," the visitor remarked.

Three Rivers pride allows no such comparisons, even when favorable. "I heered tell them Alps is mighty pretty but they ain't a patch on Glacier Peak and some of our'n. Heist yoreself out and see, if'n you don't believe me."

The good-natured flatland furriner laughed and said he might just do that on his next trip, then went back to the city and dreamed of the picturesque, winding valley that had captivated his heart. Yet he contrasted modern conveniences with life in Three Rivers and weakened. Could he give up pavement for one long main street with few automobiles, a street often dusty by the passage of mule teams and rutted and muddy in winter? He considered exchanging luxurious stores for Jake Lieberman's General Store that carries everything from groceries to glue, harness to hats, patent medicine to writing paper. Two saloons exude the unpleasant aroma of stale beer kegs and bottled spirits. Instead of a symphony, Three Rivers rings with the honest sound of hammer on anvil at the combination blacksmith shop and livery stable as the village smithy fits balky mules and skittish horses with new shoes.

"I did like getting a shave and haircut for twenty-five cents," the tempted city man reflected. "And that meal at Biddy Reed's rooming house nearly made up for the lack of other amenities." His mouth watered as he remembered tender roast beef, baked potatoes, homemade hot biscuits with honey, fresh vegetables, and especially the enormous wedge of freshly baked blueberry pie. No Seattle restaurant offered finer food. Yet when all things were taken into consideration the love of creature comforts outweighed the sense of adventure and he contented himself with annual visits.

If he had talked at greater length with the same long-time resident who scoffed at the idea the Alps could overshadow *his* mountains, he might have been entertained by the following soliloquy.

"Shore, it's a mite inconvenient when the wind blows down trees across the dirt road and makes it hard getting in and out, but being at the end of the Pleasant Valley Railroad line means we ain't stranded. That little old red depot's seen a whole lot of folks waiting for the Galloping Goose — that's our train — 'specially when the road's washed out. 'Sides, we got most everything we need right here. Two whole rooms in the schoolhouse now. A feller or gal can go clean through eighth grade. If any of 'em hankers for high school, why, the Galloping Goose runs both ways. Three Rivers is a mighty sociable town. Most of us 'tend church faithfullike." At this point he likely pauses for a moment of reverence while glancing toward the little white church and beckoning steeple. A short distance from Main Street, its spire seems to point the way to heaven. "Folks here have food, shelter, friends, and all God's creation spread out around 'em. What more can a man want? Doc Blanchard cures our bodies and Daddy O'Toone tends to our souls. We calkilate we're mighty blessed."

From this town the Galloping Goose had carried Jennifer Ashley away four years earlier. Now in the early summer of 1913 the "iron goose" was bringing her home, to the delight of the entire town. Three Rivers was Jenny's town, and if she had her way she would never leave it again.

One

"No more pencils, no more books, no more teachers' cranky looks."

Jennifer Ashley sang while she crammed the last of her possessions into her battered steamer trunk. After arranging a becoming hat on her luxuriant dark brown and copper-highlighted hair, she tried to fasten the brass clasps. Laughing, she admonished herself, "Such childishness, Miss Ashley, for an eighteen-year-old young lady who just graduated from high school and is on her way home." She collapsed onto the broad lid of the trunk. Although slender, the force of her five-foot, eight-inch frame proved enough to click down the lock.

Home, what a wonderful word! she thought to herself. Only the knowledge her family and friends expected her to stick it out had kept the homesick young woman doggedly studying to stay at the top of her class for these long years. Christmas and summer vacations always mingled joy and sadness. Joy

13

when she reached Three Rivers, the familiar tug at her heartstrings when she left. In between lay the fear of change. Would her beloved town be the same when she came home? Would her classmates have outgrown the fun they had and lost the bonds forged by study and play, worship and sharing? Each time she heaved sighs of relief when she anxiously considered the worst and discovered her fears were not realized.

Pink-cheeked from her struggle with the recalcitrant lock, Jenny straightened her snowy middy blouse and long dark skirt. "Bother! I'll have to wear the suit jacket, warm as it is. I don't dare open the trunk again." She caught it up along with a matching handbag, waved an airy goodbye to the room in which she'd lived the last four years, and walked outside to wait for her ride to the train, courtesy of a classmate's brother's vintage automobile.

"I'll be glad to get away from him, too," she muttered. "I like young men but only God knows none of them here compares well with Alvin." Her heart suddenly beat faster. Alvin Thomas had been Jenny's first boyfriend and she still preferred him to the others who longed to be her beau. Two years older than Jenny, he had been visiting some distant relatives the last time she was in Three Rivers.

"Will they never come?" Jenny complained, but her usual sunny nature permitted little petulance. Minutes later, after her friends had deposited her at the railway station and she had waved her last goodbye, she found herself exulting in the sound of the mournful train whistle. As if to urge the train to a faster speed, Jenny leaned forward at the edge of her seat. A change of trains an hour later was followed by a short wait that to Jenny seemed interminable. At last the Galloping Goose chugged into sight.

"You dear train!" she whispered. Beloved of all Three Rivers residents, the Galloping Goose not only brought in supplies but also transported the harvest of prime timber to the sawmills on Puget Sound. Rail service was provided by the Pleasant Valley Railroad Company every day except Sunday.

She boarded, torn between wanting to see friends and the need to have this time to herself. Usually the passenger coach was at least two-thirds full with folks dressed in their finest for a visit to the city. Today not many passengers rode and Jenny unobtrusively slipped into a seat at the rear. A strange fancy that she sat between two worlds filled her. Behind lay the city. She relived her bewilderment when she first arrived in that new and unfriendly world. Thousands of people scurried aimlessly in different directions, bumping and pushing each other into doorways of concrete buildings; only scraps of sky could be seen in between the towering spires.

And those funny little trolley cars! With bells clanging loudly, these odd vehicles leaped and bounced down cobblestone streets that bore no resemblance to the trails she knew and loved. Large department stores that would hold a half-dozen General Stores attracted a steady stream of customers; theatres proclaimed their attractions with a myriad of colored lights dancing across ornate facades.

Yet despite the obvious charms of the city, Jenny felt she had finished that chapter in her life. No longer gripped by the past, yet wanting to prolong the excitement of actually arriving home, Jenny fondly surveyed her surroundings and the passenger coach. Each time she rode the Galloping Goose, she never tired of what she saw. To her loving eyes, the coach was a thing of beauty. Adorned with fancy, Victorian-type gingerbread trimmings, it boasted polished brass kerosene lamps hung from the ceiling. What warmth they added when night crept into the windows! The effect was no less spectacular in daylight when each multicolored stained-glass transom reflected an array of rainbow colors across the rich plush passenger seats. A huge coal stove stood at one end of the car and kept passengers cozy in chilly weather.

Jenny patted the edge of her seat and turned her attention to her fellow travelers. There sat Mr. and Mrs. Chambers, decked out in typical go-to-the-big-city clothing. Jenny bit her lip and covered her mouth with a dainty, lace-edged handkerchief. Leave it to Mrs. Chambers to wear a flower-bedecked hat at least two inches wider than the enormous ones in style! With eight-inch hatpins to keep the gigantic bonnet in place and a fancy lace dress that would nearly sweep the floor when she stood, she nonetheless looked beautiful to Jenny.

Meek little Mr. Chambers sat with eyes forward. The correct celluloid collar so high and stiff it threatened to sever the jugular vein discouraged any movement. Jenny could only visualize his neatly pressed trousers and buttoned shoes; Mr. Chambers's ever-present derby sat jauntily on his head.

She would remember this ride as long as she lived. A wistful smile brightened her features and she relaxed, leaned her head back against the seat, and let her mind rush ahead of the clickety-clacking train wheels. Soon the dear old red depot that had seen so many happy arrivals and tearful departures would come into view.

Father would be there, Mother, perhaps Alvin if his woodswork didn't prevent him meeting her train. One dear face would be missing: Her older brother Donald had joined the merchant marine. Then an impish look made her eyes sparkle. The one person closer to her than anyone else, Laura Shipley, would let nothing stand in her way of welcoming Jenny home. The two friends had gone to the first eight grades of school together and become so inseparable that Jenny actually felt she had left half of herself behind when she went away to school. She saw the same feeling in Laura's clear blue eyes, although her friend reminded her how quickly time would pass until Christmas vacation. Jenny, the more daring, had swallowed her heartache and forced herself to respond in kind. Then she impulsively whispered, "Laura, please don't change. Don't grow up while I'm gone."

Looking back from the advanced age of eighteen, Jenny smiled at the childish request. Yet her heart warmed at Laura's quick hug and promise, "I won't, Jenny, but you mustn't either." Every vacation they had anxiously assured each other they might grow taller and become young women, but nothing else would change.

Once Jenny teasingly said, "Of course, if someday you want to become my sister instead of my best friend, I'll approve."

Laura's fair skin turned peony-red. "Shhh. Don doesn't know I exist." Yet her look of longing made Jenny clap her hands in glee and giggle when Laura hastily changed the subject.

"Threeeee Riiiiiivvvvverrrrrs!"

The conductor's call snatched Jenny from the past. The Galloping Goose slowed to a crawl and the excited girl could hardly retrieve her hand luggage from the overhead rack. She glanced out the window. What a crowd! Had the passenger coach housed an important dignitary, such as came to town once in a long while? She hadn't noticed anyone who fit the description but then she'd been so engrossed with nostalgic memories she hadn't paid much attention to all her fellow travelers.

Jenny caught up her skirt so she wouldn't trip and followed the others down the aisle. As she stepped off the train a dozen voices cried out at once. "Jenny!" "There she is!" "Welcome home, Jenny!" Happy tears sprang to her eyes. Had half of Three Rivers come to meet her?

"Father. Mother. Laura. Alvin." The names ran together in her eagerness to greet them. Her eyes opened wide. "Why, there's Jake Lieberman and Doc Blanchard. My goodness, Little Star, what are you doing in that dress? It looks like a uniform." She stared at the beautiful Indian woman she and Laura had grown up with, at the neatly braided black hair now tucked back under a white cap.

"Little Star is my nurse now," Doc Blanchard boomed. He waddled his way through the crowd and pumped Jenny's hand. Short and paunchy, with keen gray eyes that matched the thatch on his head, his appearance proclaimed both his education and compassion.

"Really? That's wonderful."

"I love it." Little Star's lustrous dark eyes glowed. "Doc Blanchard is teaching me everything I need to know to help him." An almost reverent look crossed her face and Jenny remembered how willingly the good doctor rode his horse in all kinds of weather to care for those who lived in the Indian village a few miles from town. She also remembered a story that had become legend. Shortly after Doc Blanchard chose to turn his back on city practice and riches, a colleague visited him for several weeks. He watched amazed as the doctor literally put men back together who had been injured in logging accidents, and marveled when he saw them heal. The story ran that he burst out with, "Man, how can you have such a high rate of success, considering the seriousness of many you treat?"

According to hearsay, neither confirmed nor denied by the principal party, Doc Blanchard retorted, "I work on *men,* not panty-waisted weaklings."

Jenny's mind ran double-time, with part of her greeting friends, the other remembering the times Doc had brought comfort to Donald and her when they were sick. "Remember, *I* don't heal anyone," he always reminded. "I'm just a country sawbones. If there's any healing, it comes from the Great God Almighty." His humility only added to his worth in the eyes of a town that loved him.

After the first hug, Laura had stepped back to give others a chance. Her slender, blue-clad figure, bright brown hair, and sweet face stood out against the dusty street like a cameo. Jenny longed to rush to her but her mother's training ran too deep. She must be courteous to everyone. "I'll see you soon," she finally called when her father got her luggage in the family buggy and escorted her mother and her across the street to where it sat in the shade. The buggy was hitched to the Ashley bay, Sadie, and Jenny gave the mare a loving pat before she climbed in.

Until now her homecoming had been thrilling but tranquil. In a single moment it turned to bedlam. A swarm of honeybees swept into the cluster of waving people by the little red depot. People ran and screamed, seeking shelter from the onslaught of needlelike stingers ready to inoculate those in their path.

Jenny watched from her safe vantage point across the street, torn between sympathy and mirth. Modesty was overcome by the need to escape as women fled holding ankle-length dresses halfway to their knees. Men's derby hats fell and rolled, knocked off by flailing arms. Poor old Peg Leg Johnson managed to get his stump caught in a knothole in the old boardwalk and helplessly covered his face. Soon, however, the swarm changed direction and no one got stung. "Help me up, someone," Peg Leg pleaded, then laughed at his predicament, always a good sport whose jolliness won friends.

The Ashleys wiped their eyes and then

Andrew Ashley clucked to Sadie and the buggy rolled off. Jenny treasured every turn of the wheels on the three-mile trip to the small ranch where she had lived all her life. She unconsciously strained forward and gleefully cried when the weathered log cabin came into view. She wanted to leap out and examine everything but she knew how much her homecoming meant to her parents. She thus contented herself through supper and until bedtime with catching up on all the news since Christmas vacation, as well as playing with her dog Tammy.

The next morning, however, she awakened early, donned outdoor garb, and stole quietly out of the house. She scuffed through downed leaves and inhaled the freshness of wildflowers, aware the entire forest had come to life. In the distance a woodcock rhythmically retrieved grubs from a dead cedar snag. A meadowlark's melodious mating call mingled with the chatter of a pair of gray squirrels. "You may as well get used to me. This is my forest, too," Jenny said softly. Before she turned to go she dropped to her knees on a patch of soft moss.

"Thank You, God. For —" She couldn't begin to list all the things crowding in her heart. Glad that God would understand, she simply prayed, "Thank You for everything."

Golden griddle cakes, country fresh eggs, and sweet milk awaited Jenny. Following breakfast, she helped with the dishes and tidying the house. "Mother, you've cleaned so well we won't have to do housework all summer!" To her surprise, her father didn't go directly into the fields as he normally did. Instead, Andrew lounged in a rocking chair in the big kitchen and when they finished their duties, he said, "Mother, isn't it about time for the surprise?"

Esther Ashley, an older edition of her pretty daughter, flung her apron on a chair, ready to forsake work for the pleasure of a free moment. Many times chores waited until darkness extinguished a glorious sunset's last rays or a bird had finished its song.

"What is it?" Jenny ran beside her tall father down the winding path to the barn set away from the house. "A new calf? A litter of squealing pigs?"

Esther smothered a laugh and Jenny glanced at her but learned nothing.

"Close your eyes," Andrew told her when they reached the barn. She did as she had done a hundred times before while waiting for a surprise. Her father unlatched the barn door and opened it wide.

"Open your eyes now."

Standing in a nearby stall, nickering in a low friendly tone that invited Jenny to come greet him, was the most beautiful white stallion she had ever seen. So fully absorbed was Jenny in patting the horse and getting acquainted she was only vaguely aware of the moment her parents slipped away. After saddling her magnificent surprise she led him outside. Sensing that his eagerness matched her own, she hurried to mount and together they galloped across the meadow with reckless and blissful abandon. As Jenny reined him in and stroked his strong, arched neck she told him, "You can only have one name. I christen thee White Knight. You will be my champion."

Mindful that summer brought hard work to the Ashleys, Jenny reluctantly rode back to the barn and put her mount away. She joined her gingham-clad mother who was weeding carrots and onions, shaded by a sunbonnet. Andrew painstakingly hoed the corn. The Ashleys raised all their own food and made their own butter from the milk of two cows. Hens provided fresh eggs for them and to sell. Jenny soberly thought how hard these times were for families who didn't have land to raise crops. Winter snows shut down the logging camps, the backbone of Three Rivers, but summer fires were equally debilitating. Andrew Ashley, along with many others, got in the crops, saw they were doing well, then worked for short time periods in a camp to bring in money: two and a half to three dollars a day for ten hours, with a six-day week.

Women made most of their families' clothing but shoes were a problem. Prices from one and a half to three dollars a pair meant fathers doing shoe repair work so long as soles and uppers could be held together. The town's cooperative spirit despite such deprivation was evidenced by the Ladies Aid Society that met once a month for a quilting party to tie off crazy quilts for needy families. For these reasons and more, Jenny especially treasured White Knight for she realized how her mother and father must have scrimped and saved to buy him.

Except for seeing Laura at church on Sundays, Jenny and her best friend didn't get together for several weeks. Field work required everyone's help and left little time for socializing. A few days before the Fourth of July, Esther Ashley smilingly said, "Take the rest of the day off and ride into town, dear. I know you want to see Laura and show her White Knight."

Jenny hugged her mother and enjoyed

every minute of the ride. She didn't linger in Three Rivers, although several friends called to her and her heart beat with pride because of her new horse. Red, white, and blue bunting and dozens of flags brightened the town for the upcoming celebration and potluck picnic. The line-up of events was the same each year: foot and swimming races; a greased pole climb; a greased pig contest; a baseball game between shingle weavers from Three Rivers and loggers from a neighboring town; and blaring music as the volunteer band tried to do justice to John Philip Sousa's stirring marches. Indians from the isolated camp upriver glided down the Sauk in dugout canoes, some of them to enter the crowning glory of the day, a horse race down Main Street.

Last year a tragedy had nearly occurred. One of the boys who entered the race at the shingle mill pond had no cut-off overalls, standard garb when swimming other than in seclusion. He stripped to long handle underwear and did fine to the halfway mark, but then the arms and legs stretched and he began to sink. Fortunately, a judge managed to get him out unhurt but the poor lad was nonetheless given the nickname "shitepoke," after a clumsy sand hill crane with long legs and grotesque flopping wings.

Jenny resolutely ignored the spicy cinnamon smell of cookies from Biddy Reed's and rode on. She called to Larry Benson, the U.S. Forest Service packer who stood by his string of mules next to the General Store, ready to pick up supplies for the trail camps and crows'-nests throughout his district. Andrew Ashley had once explained to his giggling daughter how the lookout fire-watcher stations came to be called crows'-nests. The name was a nautical one, indicating the perch on sailing ships' masts where a crewman kept constant vigil for icebergs and other dangers. The crows'-nests on the mountain peaks near Three Rivers offered a way to keep constant surveillance of the entire forest in an effort to detect forest fires. The hint of an idea forming in her mind gave way to sheer joy in the fluid movement of White Knight, and she forgot everything except the magnificent stallion she rode.

On a straight, half-mile stretch, Jenny loosened the reins, touched her horse's flank with her heel, and crouched low over his mane. Never had she ridden such a bolt of lightning! Yet his power kept his stride so even, she had no trouble staying on. The miles flashed by and she pulled him back to a canter, then a trot, and finally a walk.

"You glorious creature!" she exclaimed as she patted him. "I'll bet you can beat any horse in the state."

Her hand stilled. What if she, but no, it had never been done. Yet nothing said she couldn't. What would Mother and Father think? Or Alvin? Did she dare? "I'll talk it over with Laura," she told White Knight, which wasn't even winded. "Then we'll see."

TWO

"Guess what!" The sound of Jenny's voice summoned Laura from the Shipley home, followed seconds later by her parents, known affectionately to the breathless visitor as Aunt Carrie and Uncle Ben. "I'm going to ride White Knight in the Fourth of July race!"

"You aren't!" Blue-eyed Laura gasped and stepped back from Jenny. "Why, no girl or woman has ever done such a thing."

Jenny tossed her head. "What girl or woman has a horse like mine?" Mischief filled her face. "Besides, I can win, I mean, he can." She tethered White Knight to the rail fence, although he normally stood and waited if she simply dropped the reins.

Ben Shipley cocked his head and peered at the stallion. He laughed heartily. " 'Pears to me, he might just do that. What do your folks say about you riding?"

"I'm not going to tell them and don't you dare," she threatened. "I'll ride and I'll win and they'll be proud. If I say anything about it, they might protest and of course, I wouldn't ride then."

"Landsakes, child, what crazy thing will you do next!" Aunt Carrie threw her hands in the air. "Dinner's on the table. Come in and get washed."

"Yummm." Jenny did justice to thick slices of home-cured ham, hot biscuits and honey, mashed potatoes, pickled beans, and sweet milk. Shortly afterward wise Carrie Shipley shooed the two friends out of the country kitchen for a long-delayed visit.

Two hours later — after they had shared all the happenings since the last time they were together — Jenny knew the time had come. She had saved the best news for last. As Laura walked with her to the patient White Knight still munching red clover even while she mounted, Jenny bent low and whispered, "Don is coming home on leave."

Vivid red rushed into Laura's face. "And you kept it inside all the time we were talking?" she cried. "How could you?"

"I knew if I told you first, that's all we'd talk about," Jenny said practically. The telltale blush had set to rest any suspicion she had that her friend's feelings for one Donald Ashley might have changed.

"I'm glad," Laura said in a low voice but

her face gave Jenny plenty to consider on the ride home. Laura's love for Donald made Jenny's feelings for Alvin Thomas pale by comparison. Although now and then her heart thumped when she hadn't seen Alvin for a time, their good comradeship certainly didn't make her look as Laura had, radiant and eager. A strange yearning — not envy, but a new awareness of real love — crept into her heart. How could she ever have thought she'd marry Alvin? Unless her feelings changed drastically, they weren't strong enough, she realized. Strange how that one look into Laura's glorious face had shown Jenny her own heart.

"Well, I don't have to worry about it," she told White Knight, his head turned in a listening attitude. "When I meet a person God knows can complete my life and I his, I'm sure He will let me know."

Shadows from the setting sun hung low by the time Jenny reached home. How thankful she was for the long June evenings and for this country, her heritage, and her parents' decision to come to Three Rivers. The Ashleys had never had a hankering for city life. Possessed of the pioneer spirit, they endured exhausting weeks of travel by train and covered wagon until they reached Three Rivers. They then chose this secluded site for a ranch, near a river and in a valley green with life and promise. Neighbors and friendly townsfolk helped them raise their house and outbuildings and clear enough land for crops. Then came fruit trees, more land cleared of giant trees and tilled, followed by the richest harvest of all. Donald arrived and two years later, Jennifer completed their family.

At that time Three Rivers had no hospital, although a small one was later built. Doc Blanchard delivered both Donald and Jenny in the rustic Ashley home, assisted by Aunt Carrie who often served as a midwife.

Jenny looked at her home with fresh interest. The hand-hewn timber and cedar shakes came from trees that once stood in place of the three-room cottage. Nestled close beside a murmuring brook and approximately a half-mile from the foot of a snow-capped peak, at times inside the cottage she and Donald had heard thunderous reverberations when great boulders and ice chunks broke loose and crashed down from the massive glacier that never melted.

Off to one side near the brook and lower end of the orchard stood a small replica of the cottage, Pixie House. What wonderful memories Jenny had of the playhouse her father built so she and Laura, and sometimes Little Star, could have a secret place.

Donald never bothered the girls, being too absorbed in such important tasks as catching little green frogs and grasshoppers, chasing cottontails, or discovering small garter snakes. Barefoot and happy, the children cheerfully did their chores and cherished the hours free of duty, willing to suffer the stubbed toes and blackberry vine scratches so they could squish through mud puddles.

Both children loved the infrequent trips to town and the wonderful General Store with its glass jars filled with candy, a red machine that ground coffee beans, enormous bunches of bananas, and even a huge orange cat that presided over the cash register. Always Andrew or Esther let them choose one piece, plus an extra treat for Laura and Little Star. How many peppermint sticks and suckers, lemon drops and licorice had been enjoyed in the playhouse! Now she dismounted and led White Knight down the faint trail. A certain reluctance to go inside touched her, a feeling she could only describe as waiting for Laura.

"Thank goodness she promised to come over soon," Jenny confided aloud to her horse. She resolutely turned her back on the enticing little building and went to care for her horse. Yet her mind lingered on past events. Did Donald remember the wonder of prizes in boxes, the whistles, miniature revolvers, and tin soldiers? How she missed him. He had been such a good brother all her life. They seldom argued and although he had never shown extreme interest in Laura, Jenny found herself hoping this time he would.

The very next afternoon Laura appeared. Following the midday meal, the grown friends walked slowly to Pixie House, arm in arm. It hadn't changed, although they had to stoop a bit to get inside. "Let's play remember," Jenny suggested when they had seated themselves on two chairs that miraculously still held them.

"All right." If Laura preferred to discuss Don, she didn't let on. "Do you remember all the animals we used to see, even a wildcat once and a bear?" Her eyes sparkled like twin blue stars. "And sometimes when it snowed so hard and your horse Dandy couldn't make it home, do you remember how Donald stayed with us?"

"Dear old Dandy. I remember bouncing up and down on his back and clinging to Donald." Jenny went on, her eyes dreamy. "Remember dare base, pum pum pullaway, and shinny? You and I and Little Star were the only girls who'd play shinny with vine maple sticks and a small tin can. I can still feel my shins sting when some of the older boys whacked us."

"They never did when Donald played," Laura said loyally and Jenny nodded. "*I* liked when the whole Sunday school class came out here to your ranch and the mill owner, Mr. Stillman, came with his hayrack for the younger ones. He sure was a good Sunday school teacher. You never let anyone except Little Star and me play in Pixie House, though." Fond understanding shone in her eyes.

Jenny lowered her voice, although she knew they couldn't be overheard. "I'll never forget when the eighth grade boys played hooky that spring day and went swimming in the lake at the edge of the wild cranberry marsh."

Laura giggled and modestly looked away while Jenny continued. "Remember how strict Miss Douglas was? I wonder how the boys felt when they realized *their teacher* had seen them swimming without any clothes. Donald wasn't in on it but he peeped through the schoolhouse window after school."

"I remember you told me. Miss Douglas kept the boys waiting at least fifteen minutes. They fidgeted and coughed. Finally she asked if they knew why they were there. None of them lied."

Jenny took up the story. "They all said they were sorry so she told them never to be deceitful or underhanded if they wanted to be great in life and then she dismissed them."

"I never could understand why she didn't punish them," Laura mused.

"It was only a few weeks until school ended and she knew she'd never see them again. Besides, I think she really loved us all."

"Are you going to be a teacher?" Laura asked.

Jenny shook her head. "No, I have another idea." Her mother's voice calling them cut short confidences and Jenny promised, "I'll tell you later. Right now, I'm just so thankful our Heavenly Father has blessed us with this wonderful place to live, our families, and each other."

"So am I." Laura squeezed her friend's hand. "And I'm so glad Donald is coming home."

The next morning Jenny rode in with her father on a wagon to pick up oats and a sack of bran for the cows. While Andrew was at the General Store, she found her chance to visit the huge, mustachioed blacksmith. As a child she thought the man hurt the horses when he took a red-hot iron out of the flaming forge, hammered it into a half-circle around the horn on the anvil, and then cooled and nailed the perfectly formed horseshoe in place. As Jenny chatted naturally with him, she knew she had her perfect opportunity to bring up the Fourth of July race.

"It's going to be a dandy," the blacksmith told her. "I hear there are some mighty fine pieces of horseflesh entered. I always like the race better than anything except maybe the picnic." His huge frame shook. "I do like good food and there's always enough to feed Three Rivers and half the county. No better cooks anywhere, either," he added.

As he continued to describe with mouth-watering accuracy the contents of a few picnic baskets, Jenny found her mind wandering off. So White Knight had some competition, did he? She shrugged off a niggling little thought but it darted back again. Suppose she entered the race and lost. How humiliating that would be. Yet she'd trust her stallion to do his best. She wouldn't quit just because other good horses would run.

"It wouldn't be much of an honor beating a bunch of nags the speed of Sadie, would it, boy?" Jenny told her horse later that afternoon. White Knight whinnied and threw back his head. She couldn't help laughing, he sounded so indignant at her suggestion. Their long rides had shown Jenny his superb strength and endurance and she'd learned all his unique mannerisms. Anyway, riding in the race would be fun. She'd make sure of that.

Jenny ran into a snag that very evening. After supper Esther remarked, "I'm so glad we finished your new pink lawn, dear. It makes you look like a wild rose. I suppose you'll wear it to the celebration?"

"Why —" Jenny didn't know what to say. She certainly couldn't ride White Knight wearing the fluffy confection she and her mother had worked so hard making. Looking like a wild rose wouldn't help win the Fourth of July race.

"I thought I'd ride to town instead of going with you in the buggy," she faltered.

"She wants everyone to see her new horse," Andrew put in. His eyes twinkled. "We can take her dress with us. I'm sure Biddy Reed will let Jenny change there."

Jenny's heart settled back to its normal beat. She would never lie to her parents but the Shipleys had kept her secret and so far, no one else knew of her daring plan. "That's perfect," she approved. "That way I can wear my riding skirt and a clean middy blouse so White Knight will know who's riding him and have my pretty new dress for in town." She didn't add that it would require some extra changing clothes and taking Biddy into her confidence.

On the morning of the Fourth, the Ashleys rose early. Independence Day it might be, but cows and chickens and horses had to be fed. Jenny curried White Knight until he shone like the snowy satin of a bride's gown. "Even if we don't win the race, you'll be the best looking horse entered," she whispered in the stallion's ear. He tossed his head and nudged her shoulder with his soft nose. A little later, when she mounted, she took note that her new dress and a pair of dressy shoes had been carefully packed in individual boxes to survive the trip to town. "See you soon," she called gaily, waved, and rode off, conscious of her parents' loving gaze. "Thank You, God, for the best family in the whole world," she prayed, then settled back and urged White Knight into the easy canter that ate up the miles without tiring him or Jenny.

Straight for Biddy Reed's rooming house she headed, once she had tethered her horse in a nearby shady area and given him a sparing drink of water while removing road dust from his gleaming sides. "Rest," she ordered. "We want to do our best." A few minutes later she smiled at her looking-glass image. The dress matched the flags of excitement in her cheeks. The intricate tucks on the bodice, the result of many long evenings' work, had truly been fashioned with love. Again Jenny thanked God for her wonderful mother and simply added, "Help me not to be disappointed if I don't win, and help me to ride well."

Jenny stepped outside, after thanking the motherly Biddy Reed who beamed on her. "Hello, Mr. Grimsley," she called to the dour man who was headed out of town, unlike the rest of the countryside,

"Howdy." The grudging greeting held little friendliness but Jenny didn't mind. As far back as she could remember, the children had called him "Mean Mr. Grimsley." Sam Grimsley *was* mean, Jenny reflected, when without another word he strode away. He never allowed a child near his place and often made strange sounds to frighten them away. One winter he even put ashes from his coal stove on the town's favorite coasting hill that lay close to his humble abode. Some of the boys retaliated by throwing rocks at his shack.

Jenny felt sorry for Sam Grimsley because she knew his only friends were Daddy O'Toone, Doc Blanchard, and, of course, her family. He must be lonely, but he doesn't let anyone get to know him, she thought. An idea started to form in her mind, but the Fourth of July didn't lend itself to plotting on behalf of even one crotchety man. Jenny skipped a little from sheer exuberance and went off to find Laura.

She discovered her friend, gowned in the blue she loved so much, talking with Little Star. Although the young Indian woman usually wore clothes like her schoolmates, in honor of the holiday she had chosen a native costume. Soft buckskin, deeply fringed and intricately trimmed with beads, highlighted her dusky face and shining dark eyes and hair. A beaded band around her forehead anchored an eagle's feather and Jenny remembered her friend's grandfather had been called Eagle Feather.

"Anyone here I know?"

The beloved voice whipped Jenny around and brought a quick blush to Laura's face. "Don!" Jenny threw her arms around her brother. "When did you get here?"

"Just now." His teasing gaze turned from one to the other. "Well, the three maidens from Three Rivers are certainly growing up!" Jenny saw how his laughing gaze lingered longest on Laura. Any man should see the quiet young woman's worth; Jenny hoped Donald would have sense enough to recognize it soon.

Alvin Thomas, ruddy-faced and pleasant-looking, joined them, then a half-dozen other young men and women who had grown up together and enjoyed each other's company. They laughed until they ached, watching one man and boy after another try to climb the greased pole. One of the young women who had just moved to town innocently asked, "How do they get it greased the first time?"

"Simple," Don told her. "A man climbs it with a gunny sack dipped in axle grease and simply greases the pole as he slides down. For what it's worth, there's a five-dollar bill on top," he added.

The greased pig race proved even more hilarious. A big porker, shiny with grease, raced up one street and down another, followed by a yelling crowd. Time after time, an intrepid participant tackled the pig, only to have him squish out between his hands. The smart man who won the pig as a prize grabbed him square around the middle, hung on for dear life, and ignored the frenzied squeals until the judges declared the pig his. A good-natured friend produced a length of rope and helped truss the pig's legs. He allowed that he'd laughed so hard he couldn't hold the pig when he had his hands on it.

Jenny held her sides, trying to get her breath. Yet all through the games and races, her secret prompted an exchange of looks with Laura and innocent comments that set them laughing again, to the complete mystification of the rest of their crowd.

At noon long tables, constructed by laying boards on sawhorses, sagged with the weight of Three Rivers's best cooking. Early roasting ears of corn flanked chicken, beef, and venison. Pink hams and a rainbow of every kind of salad known elbowed up to apples pies, cinnamon buns, and at least twenty-five cakes, each one different. Jenny ate heartily. The baseball game still lay ahead, with the horse race last. She would work off the heavy meal long before it was time to ride.

Bang! "My goodness, what's that?" Laura gasped.

Don and the other young men pelted toward the sound and came back howling. "One of the flatland furriners had something more than punch to drink. He was waving around a skyrocket and it got too close to his smoking cigar. Then, boom!"

"The only thing wrong with our celebrations is having some people drink," Jenny said disgustedly. She watched the happy groups of grownups greeting one another and exchanging gossip, news, and recipes. Barefoot boys with dust-streaked faces ran to and fro "shooting up" the town with their cap guns. Little girls tooted horns between taking licks of rapidly melting ice cream cones. A booming voice from a bunting-draped dais announced the events of the day. Visiting dignitaries made speeches to which few listened. Martial music displayed the long hours put in by the volunteer band.

Almost oblivious to the colorful festivities, Jenny moved about in a daze, consumed by the race of her life.

Three

The assemblage drifted toward the shingle mill for log-rolling and swimming races. This year something new awaited them. The baggage man from the Galloping Goose startled the town by diving from a sixty-foot-high elevator, normally used for stacking shingle bolts, into the mill pond! Obviously savoring his moment of glory, he poised on the platform, silhouetted against the blue sky, then straight as an arrow he dove, entering the water with hardly a splash. He received a hearty round of applause before the crowd headed for the local baseball diamond to see the annual game between arch rivals. The Galloping Goose didn't run on holidays but the Pleasant Valley Railroad had graciously allowed the visiting team to borrow equipment used by gandy dancers in maintaining the roadbed: a couple of hand cars and a push car. Large and muscular, the men on both teams could almost drive a ball into the next county, but couldn't run for sour apples. Occasionally, they chose a small, fleet-footed boy to circle the bases when they made a hit.

Halfway through the hotly contested game with the score at 2-2, a big logger marched to the plate while a wiry barefoot boy in knee pants crouched ready to run. Jeers from the visitors only brought a collective grin to hometown rooters. This boy could run like a deer.

The pitcher hurled a fast ball, and then came a mighty swing. "St-e-e-rike!"

Another fast ball enticed a ruthless, more powerful swing. "St-e-e-rike!"

The batter pulled his cap lower over his eyes and set his jaw squarely. The pitch hissed across the plate. *Crack.* The dead center hit easily cleared the center field fence. The runner streaked for first base and headed for second, curly hair shining in the sun, the love of running all over his face. Suddenly the large button holding up his pants came off. Down they came. The child reached for them but Doc Blanchard roared from the sidelines, "Never mind the pants! Keep on running!"

The boy loved Doc and never questioned his barked instructions. He jumped out of his breeches and finished circling the bases for a home run, to the embarrassment of the girls and women and the delight of the home team. Jenny felt torn between the desire to giggle and the need to keep a straight face, especially when the ingenuous child returned for his pants, donned them, and scurried off the field. His persistence appeared to inspire his brawny logger friends as the game ended in a 7-5 victory for the hometown.

Jenny slipped away during the final cheers. She must hurry and change. Her flying feet landed at Biddy Reed's now-deserted rooming house and her fingers felt like eight extra thumbs when she slipped from her dress into her riding skirt, middy, and boots. She had decided to ride bareheaded, so she quickly caught her lustrous hair back in one thick braid before running outside to her beloved White Knight.

Main Street in Three Rivers, the site of the race, lay wide and dusty. The race itself was only one-quarter of a mile and from town to the first bend in the road was approximately three-quarters of a mile. Contestants thus had ample room to bring their horses to a gradual stop. People lined the street several deep, awaiting the two-heat race. Jenny knew riders often held back their horses in the first heat to fool the onlookers and win side bets. She scorned such dishonesty and the practice of gambling. Money should be used wisely, not thrown away on bets.

She mounted and turned White Knight toward the starting line.

"Get off the street, please, miss," a judge from a neutral town called respectfully. "We're ready to start the race."

"I know." She maneuvered into position just behind the line.

"But then you're a girl! Young ladies don't ride in this race." The judge's eyes popped out and his face turned red.

"I saw nothing in the rules that says I can't compete." Jenny's heart pounded but she kept her voice cool, seeing the wide grin on Donald's face, the anxiety in Laura's eyes, and the uncertainty on her parents' faces.

"No woman has ever ridden in the Fourth of July race," the judge bellowed.

"Let her ride," someone called.

"There ain't no rule says she can't." A wave of approval filled the air and the judge acquiesced. Jenny noticed the open mouths of some of the women and their disapproving stares. She proudly raised her head. God had given her a strong body and a beautiful horse. No narrow-minded person could deprive her of her right to do what she loved, especially when she caught the tiny nod from her mother that meant "go ahead" and saw her father's twinkling eyes.

She took her place. "Get set," the starter ordered, his pistol pointing upward. *Bang!* He fired and the race began.

Spectators craned their necks but Jenny paid them little attention. White Knight had leaped forward as a spring released. She bent low over his mane. "Run, you wonderful horse!" She heard yelling and the pounding of hooves behind her but none came near. Her lips curled. They must be holding back, perhaps thinking White Knight would be so winded he couldn't run the second heat well. A delighted grin tilted her lips up. She hadn't even let her horse out yet! She'd simply allowed him to run fast enough to keep in front of the others.

They flashed across the finish line to the amazed cheers of the crowd and Jenny slowed to a canter, then a trot, and finally a walk. She noticed the little group of male competitors huddled and gesticulating during the time it took to get back to the starting line for the second heat. Her keen eyes ferreted out a certain furtive look between two who had come in from another town.

"They're up to something," she breathed

into White Knight's ear. "We'll show them." He flicked his ear and waited while she patted him, listening for the signal.

Bang! Did White Knight sense what she knew? He lunged like a juggernaut and put two lengths between his heels and the closest rival, gaining momentum with every leap. When he crossed the finish line for the second time, white vapor came from his nostrils and he was a full four lengths ahead of the rest of the field.

The baggage man's high dive had become a faint memory as the frenzied crowd cheered the daring young woman and her magnificent steed. Jenny slowly rode back, glad to see that any earlier hesitancy in her parents' faces had changed to pride and admiration. White Knight trotted to the judges' stand. Even the man who had objected beamed and cried "Well done!" when he placed a wreath of flowers on the horse's neck and handed Jenny a blue silk ribbon and the twenty-five-dollar cash prize. The crowd continued to yell until Jenny rode away to the livery stable, a better place to rub down White Knight. Not until he had cooled down and been watered — and given a handful of oats — would Jenny leave and go back to the rooming house.

Kindly Biddy Reed greeted her. "Child,

child, what a ride! Now, I have hot water and you can use my room. I near had a heart attack when I saw you come riding up to the judges' stand but I'm glad. No reason a young lady can't show up the boys once in a while."

Jenny made short work of her toilette and again gowned in pink, she rejoined her friends. By the time a pick-me-up supper magically appeared on the long tables for anyone not still stuffed from dinner, half the town had congratulated her. Andrew and Esther Ashley climbed in the buggy and headed home but Don and Jenny planned to stay overnight at the Shipleys. The evening fireworks display was not to be missed. While Little Star left to help Doc with the inevitable firecracker accidents, friends drifted off in couples until only Jenny and Alvin and Laura and Donald remained. The fiery pinwheels, colored roman candles, and skyrockets soaring into the air and exploding into fantastic star-fountains of red, white, and blue elicited the all-too-predictable oohs and ahs from their cozy group.

The last burst of fireworks, a gorgeous replica of an American flag, was accompanied by the band's stirring rendition of "America." As hundreds of voices joined in, a strange and unexplainable sadness kept

Jenny from singing.

Her perfect day was over. Yet as the sun slipped behind the mountains leaving in its stead a star-studded sky, Jenny knew she would always have this day and other happy memories to come, as numerous as the lights above.

Hours earlier a stranger to Three Rivers stood to one side of the throng and wondered what the future held for him. He was a good six-feet tall and strikingly handsome without being effeminate or what some might consider too perfect. A tanned complexion showcased his short, curly blond hair and bright blue eyes, and wide shoulders and a lean but muscular physique bespoke his natural athleticism.

"Well, Burgess." A hand clapped down on his shoulder. "Think you'll like Three Rivers?"

Keith turned and smiled at Larry Benson. "Sure, but I won't be seeing much of it this summer."

The weathered face broke into a grin. "It's a long way from here to your crows'-nest on top of Pinnacle Peak. Many a man I've packed into the headwaters of the Sauk. Some haven't been able to handle the loneliness of being a lookout firewatcher."

"How can anyone be lonely in the forest?"

Keith was genuinely astonished. "After a year of studies I can't wait to get out into God's creation."

"Glad you feel that way." Larry beamed and Keith knew he'd made a friend. "You planning to be a forest ranger?"

"Someday. It's all I ever wanted to do." Keith remembered his awe when he learned he could choose to spend his life outdoors. Trees and birds and flowers, animals and lakes and sky attested to the wonder of God's goodness. Keith had committed his life to Christ years before and felt as close to his Creator and Savior in the mountains as when he attended church. He couldn't help suspecting that God loved mountains, too, or He wouldn't have made them so beautiful.

"Are you joining in the games?" Larry wanted to know.

"Not this time. I thought I'd just watch. This is my first trip to this area." Keith looked around the little town hovering in its nest of hills and peaks. "I hope someday I can get assigned here. I wouldn't mind spending the rest of my life in Three Rivers if it's as friendly as it seems today."

"It is. Oh, there's the usual bickering, but mostly without malice." Larry shrugged. "Saturday nights are pretty wild but as more and more family folk come in, that will change. It's a good place to live. I was born here."

Keith's brown hand shot out and fastened on the packer's strong wrist. *"Who is that girl?"* He nodded toward a group across the street.

"The one in blue is Laura Shipley, she's real nice. Big Bear's daughter Little Star is wearing buckskin. Wonder why Big Bear isn't here today?"

Keith couldn't have cared less. "And the one in pink?"

"Jenny Ashley. Her brother Don's just joined them, home on leave from the merchant marine."

A hail from down the street called Larry away but Keith stood rooted to the spot, his attention focused on the young woman called Jenny. *The Pink Lady.* Keith grinned sheepishly at his mental flight of fancy. Yet something about the tall but graceful figure, the wild rose color in her cheeks and her dark brown hair with its copper gleams so tastefully arranged, left him breathless. For a moment her laughing dark gaze turned his way but their eyes did not meet.

"How can I talk to her?" he muttered. The town's informality might not stretch to a strange young man casually marching up to one of its fairest daughters and begging her acquaintance. *I haven't been this smitten since I was ten years old and fell in love with the little redheaded girl who moved in next door,* he confessed to himself. *Who says there's no such thing as love at first sight?*

All afternoon he managed to catch glimpses of Jenny Ashley and still remain inconspicuous. He even saw the way she looked at one of the young men in her party. *Don't be a fool,* he told himself scowling. *Did you think a young woman like that would just be sitting around waiting for you to come along?* Young women in these mountain towns married early. She must be about eighteen. Just right for a twenty-three-year-old man like himself.

"Whoa, boy, you're going way too fast," he warned and felt idiotic when a nearby horse neighed and shied away from him.

The dinner he ate could have been bread and ambrosia instead of mashed potatoes, baked beans, jam and jelly, pickles, meat, salad, and dessert. Even the ice cream, packed in rock salt in enormous wooden freezers and shipped in for the occasion, had little appeal. How could he meet Jenny without being forward?

He still hadn't solved his problem when the announcer called for the horse race contestants to line up. Busy searching for Jenny, he missed the commotion at the judges' stand until a loud voice protested, "Young ladies don't ride in this race."

When Jenny answered in her lovely, bell-like voice, "I saw nothing in the rules that says I can't compete," Keith felt himself turn warm with indignation. Without considering anything except the belligerent judge, he called, "Let her ride," and he laughed joyously when the crowd took up his cry. Yet when the race began, his cheering died on his lips. She looked so small, hunched over the huge white stallion's neck. He opened his mouth to cry "Jenny, don't do it!" and clamped his lips shut. Why should he care so much for a young woman he had never met, with whom he had never exchanged a word?

Chest tight, hands clenched, he heard the starting gun and saw the cloud-white horse leap forward. Dust spurted from the horses' hooves. Keith paid no attention. He stayed silent, marveling at this skilled horsewoman, even when he wanted to yell, "Come on, Jenny. Win!" If and when he met her she must not have an uncouth memory of him. She would be Miss Ashley, outwardly at least.

"She did it!" A total stranger pounded

Keith on the back and he came out of his reverie. "She sure did," he enthusiastically agreed. "Now if she can just do it again."

Along with hundreds of others he watched the entrants return and again line up. Keith narrowed his eyes when he saw the scheming look between two contestants. Did she notice? He couldn't tell, although her face had been turned toward the riders. She leaned forward, grace in every movement. Again the pistol fired. Keith relaxed. Jenny and her horse had leaped ahead of the field and any possibility of foul play. This time he couldn't hold back the cheers, knowing they would be lost in the roar of approval. One of their own — "an' a gurl, at that!" an old-timer hollered — had taken the prize.

Only the presence of the young man someone called Alvin restrained the new lookout man from rushing over to congratulate the winner. The proprietary way the beaming swain respectfully took Jenny's arm held Keith back. He went through the rest of the celebration in an uncertain mood and left town the next day for his new job. Riding a pack mule fourteen miles up a dusty trail in scorching weather tested the novice's mettle. Every cutback also took him farther from Jenny. He casually waited a few miles then asked Larry Benson, who jogged along in front of him, "What did you think of the race?"

"Great, but then Jennifer Ashley's special." Larry went on to confirm that Alvin Thomas was her longtime boyfriend and had the "inside track." Two months on Pinnacle Peak meant no chance at all to meet her, Keith thought morosely. Mile after mile he swayed awkwardly atop the old mule, eating dust and soothing his pounding muscles. When Larry called a halt by a small stream, Keith tumbled off his mule and drank the icy water until his teeth ached. They stayed at the pack train watering place just long enough for man and beast to satisfy their thirst then pushed on. Three miles lay ahead, two of them up the steep mountain. Keith followed Larry's instructions to let the mule have his head when they came to places where the trail had been built across dangerous terrain.

The end of the trail — the place where supplies got unloaded — finally appeared. To reach his crows'-nest home, Keith must climb the last twenty feet on a rope ladder. The peak had originally been so small that workers blasted off twenty-five feet to make it wide enough for a ten by twelve-foot building. Drenched with perspiration, the men hoisted the supplies up with a wind-lass. Once everything was shipshape, Larry told Keith goodbye and left.

Keith stood looking out the windows of his new home. He could see a hundred miles in some directions. He'd bet at night he could actually touch the stars. "Dear God, I'm here at last. This summer will tell me if I'm fit for forest ranger work." His heart thrilled even as he yawned. The long ride plus the 8,000-foot elevation had drained his strength. He ate a hurried meal and readied himself for bed. Yet the strangeness of his surroundings and the memory of Jenny Ashley combined to leave him wakeful. For a long time he sat looking into the heavens, feeling as the psalmist David had when he gazed into the sky and realized the magnitude of God, and the smallness of humankind.

"To think that You, Almighty and Ever-lasting, cared enough about this world to send Your Son to die and save those who believe and accept Him!" Keith spoke aloud, something he knew he would do many times in the next two months. His heart swelled within him. Could any man be more blessed?

Still sleepless, he reviewed the day's con-versation with Larry. The U.S. Forest Service was in the midst of building a network of horse trails throughout the district for fire protection. The three mountains selected for crows'-nests had been carefully weighed for merit and chosen because of their strategic locations. The combined efforts of the crows'-nest observers meant knowledge of the entire forest district. Like Pinnacle Peak, the Liberty Bell tower stood about 8,000 feet high. Keith shivered, glad he hadn't drawn that assignment. Liberty Bell could only be reached by traversing a huge and icy glacier. The year before, a man had lost his footing and slid over 300 feet. His backpack saved his life when a shoulder strap caught on a jagged, jutting rock a few yards from a sheer thousand-foot drop-off. Although rescued, severe injuries prevented him from working.

The third lookout, Flower Dome, lived up to its lovely name. A short distance above the timberline, to reach its 5,000-foot aerie required only about two hours of strenuous hiking up a steep, winding trail, well worth the effort for the view from the crows'-nest. It had been erected at the edge of a large meadow waist-deep in wildflowers that bloomed all summer.

Keith yawned again and stretched. "Well, Lord, unlike most jobs, I'm starting at the

top in this one and working my way down!"
With a final look into the spangled sky, he
crawled into bed and slept dreamlessly, a
strong man at peace with God, himself, and
his world.

Four

Long before automobiles and steam donkeys, Three Rivers had won its reputation as a rough but thriving frontier town. Two mills, lumber and shingle, hummed with activity and several mining outfits flourished in the nearby hills. Scores of wagons hauled ore and lumber to the railroad siding for shipment to the city. Pack mule strings constantly plodded to the mines. Dusty, tired men whooped it up in saloons; tinhorn gamblers brought on the inevitable fracas, as did belligerent drunks. Bartenders ended such scraps by letting the culprits have it over the head with a stout stick, while the battle-scarred piano player continued tinkling the ivories as if nothing had happened.

Tough men in a tough country, they fought at the slightest provocation then turned around and shared everything they had with anyone in distress. Besides the loggers, millworkers, and miners, specially skilled rivermen, or bolt drivers, added their talents to the logging business.

During the summer loggers felled and bucked (cut) giant cedars into short lengths called shingle bolts (the larger ones were split in half) in the forest along the banks of Sauk River. Teams of horses hauled these shingle bolts by wooden sled to the river's edge, where they eventually were floated downstream to the Three Rivers shingle mill. During the course of the journey many bolts would lodge on huge river boulders. Indians capable of handling dugout canoes laughed at danger and dislodged the bolts — sometimes in icy water up to their armpits — and literally "drove" them. Bolt drives usually came in early spring during the rainy season when plenty of water meant hiring fewer men. Some of Donald and Jenny's most exciting memories surrounded their excursions to the bolt drives, each clinging to Andrew Ashley's hand and standing back out of the way to watch the action.

The Ashleys also loved the seasons when the Sauk, Suiattle, and "Stilly" (Stilliguamish) rivers teemed with steelhead and giant salmon. For centuries massive runs of fish migrated to the upper reaches of the river to deposit their eggs in shallow gravel riverbeds. Once hatched, the fingerlings made their run to the sea for a period of four years. These adult salmon then returned to the same spot they had been hatched and completed the life cycle.

Because Jenny and her family were good friends with Little Star and her father, Big Bear, the Ashleys were always welcome among the Indian people. From childhood Jenny appreciated the proud Native Americans whose ancestors had cultivated and cared for a land abounding with wild berries, succulent roots, giant salmon, and game. She never tired of watching the Indians stand motionless in their dugouts, their spears upraised. The Ashleys had been treated to a wide variety of wild game as Big Bear enjoyed visiting and seldom came without a gift. Donald liked venison jerky best, narrow strips that were dried until hard.

Most of all the Ashleys liked their Indian friends' stories. The younger generation spoke English well but the older tribe members usually conversed in broken English. Donald never tired of hearing old Johnny Jim's tale of hunting with Billy Two Horse. After the usual greeting of "Klahowya" (howdy) he related his story.

"We go way up Suiattle, kill goat on Green Mountain. Clean, good, set down for rest. Set twenty minutes on side of hill above lake. See bear swim 'cross lake. No want kill, so leave gun Billy Two Horse. Me go down hill to lake where bear he come out. He biggest bear me ever see, hi-yu skookum [big, strong]. Me go way, bear he come after me. Me go faster, him come fast, too. Me no have gun so get hunting knife out of belt.

"Bear he stand up, fight like man. Him plenty good. Me try kill, bear grab hand. Me try other hand, bear grab. Me tired, try last time, knife hit him jaw. Me no can pull knife, so hold on hard. Knife break, bear go way. Four year later me go hunting same place. See big bear, good for teepee, so kill. When skin, find piece hunting knife in jaw. Me feel good. Him no more hi-yu skookum bear try kill Johnny Jim."

Donald and Jenny never knew whether to believe the story but just seeing the old man chuckle and slap his leg over his incredible tale brought them enjoyment.

The days following the Fourth of July slipped by, each filled with the joy of being young and alive in a world scented with wildflowers and warmed by friendship. When Laura came to the Ashley ranch to spend a week, she and Jenny did all the things once again they had done as children.

Pixie House lured them, as it always had, not just as a playhouse but as a place to share solemn secrets.

One shimmering afternoon when the little refuge offered coolness under its protective maple, Laura asked, "Remember when I dropped your doll Judy and broke her arm?"

Jenny blinked then laughed at such a childish but poignant memory. "I'll never forget it. You felt worse than I did. I remember that you cried and I didn't."

Laura's blue eyes seemed to darken against her ivory complexion. A bronzed visage was not the feminine ideal, a fact sometimes lost on Jenny when she forgot to wear her sunbonnet in the field. "Now that we're grown up, I'll tell you why. My parents were so poor I never had a doll. I couldn't tell even you, I was too ashamed. Judy, with her porcelain arms and legs and face, was almost a real person to me."

Jenny stared at her beloved friend and a quick rush of tears crowded behind her eyelids. Without a moment's hesitation, she crossed to a wooden box her father had made long ago, opened it, and reached inside. Silently she took out a small bundle wrapped in a pink blanket and handed it to Laura.

Her friend's eyes widened. Laura unwrapped the still-lovely porcelain doll with a scar on its arm where her mother had glued it together years ago. "Dear Judy, how I loved you!" She held the doll close and managed a shaky laugh. "Now I don't know who feels better, me for a precious gift or you for giving it."

A loud scratching interrupted the tender moment. "That's Tammy." Jenny scrambled to open the door and her black and white border collie bounded in. When Tammy cocked her head with an expression that asked if they weren't going to play with her, Laura and Jenny laughingly acquiesced and together went into the forest, Laura still holding Judy.

"Come back here, Tammy," Jenny sternly called when the dog chased after a cottontail. "Just because border collies inherit the instinct to herd sheep and other livestock, every time she sees a bunny she tries to round it up," she explained to Laura.

"Has she learned any new tricks?"

"Not since I got home. I've been too busy," Jenny admitted.

"Tammy barked like crazy the first time she saw me," Don interjected as he snuck up on them. Although taller, he and Jenny resembled one another in coloring and with their slim, graceful bodies.

"Why shouldn't she?" Jenny pretended to be indignant. "You haven't been home since I got her."

"She likes me now," he boasted and proved it by snapping his fingers and calling the dog, which leaped into his arms and licked his face.

Laughing, they walked on, along a little used cow trail until a fragile barrier stopped them. A huge orange spider had diligently spun a silken web, intertwining gossamer strands of silver into a masterpiece. Although Jenny and Laura both hated spiders, the perfection of the web caused them to turn back and leave it unbroken. Donald teased them, but good-naturedly left the spider to finish the job.

"Jenny." Laura stopped short, her cheeks pinkened above the white collar of her simple dress. At that moment Jenny saw the way Don looked at her. "Tomorrow night is the Literary Society meeting and it's talent night. Why don't you have Tammy perform? She's so good."

"Not a bad idea," Don confirmed. "Sure glad there's a meeting while I'm home. I miss the newspaper, though." He sighed, but his eyes twinkled. "After all, the L.S. was begun to keep the townspeople informed, even if only a typewritten sheet of paper posted in the General Store." He threw back his head and his laugh echoed. "I heard it stopped because folks learned the local gossips were always ahead of the paper."

"At least the monthly meetings continue," Jenny told him. "What's the prize this time?"

Laura shook her head. "Whatever's donated. It could be a homemade quilt, a box of groceries, a wagonload of wood. Once someone won a round trip to the city on the Galloping Goose!" She bounced a little with anticipation then blushed when Don grinned at her. "I hear there's a really good lineup of talent but Tammy's as good as any of them."

"We'll be there." Jenny called her dog and gently pulled the silky ears and patted her head. "Think we can win?"

"Woof!" Tammy promptly barked and sat up.

All the next day between chores the young women and Donald put Tammy through her repertoire of tricks: zigzagging between Donald's legs while he was walking ("You'll have to do that with her because I'll be wearing a dress," Jenny warned); sitting up and folding her paws then bowing her head as if in prayer; looking in the mirror and putting her head between her front paws when Jenny told her she had a dirty face, and many others. Usually the older Ashleys didn't make it in for Literary Society because staying up until midnight Saturday made it that much harder to get up and go to church on Sunday. However, this time they made an exception.

Jenny's heart sank when she saw the competition. George Coleman tuned up his fiddle in one corner. His rare ability to play the instrument left-handed was so highly developed folks said they could almost hear the old turkey gobble when he plunged into the toe-tapping "Turkey in the Straw." Beth White, a vocal soloist, cleared her throat and sang a few tentative warm-up notes. Clancy Kramer shuffled his feet in the first intricate steps of the clog dance that made him famous.

As the evening's program began, each in turn performed. Jenny, Donald, and Tammy gave a performance so faultless even the other contestants clapped their approval and ungrudgingly watched the Ashley trio accept first prize: an enormous cheese wheel donated by Jake Lieberman.

"It's a good thing I spent time with Laura when I first got home," Jenny confided to her mother one sunny afternoon when Don inveigled Laura into taking a walk. "Don's taken over and I don't see him inviting his sister along."

"I thought it's what you wanted."

"Why, Mother!" Jenny dropped the dishtowel she'd been using. "How did you know?"

Esther Ashley's warm brown eyes glowed just like her daughter's. "It's quite obvious, dear." She glanced around the kitchen and lowered her voice. "Since there's no one here but Tammy, I'll tell you a secret. Don had a long talk with your father and me last night. He said all these years he had loved Laura but didn't realize it until he came home and saw how sweet and womanly she'd grown. He's troubled because he has to leave for Seattle to board ship in a few days. Should he tell Laura he's in love with her, or wait until he earns the captain's rating he's worked so hard to obtain? Or should he forget the captain's stripes and ask her to marry him now?"

"It's a big decision." Jenny's warm heart ached over her brother's dilemma. She stared unseeingly out the kitchen window. "But then, so is marriage. Mother, how does a girl, a woman, ever really know when she meets the man she should marry?"

A glorious look of confidence made Esther's face even more beautiful. "My dear child, no one can tell you *how* you will know, just that you will." If Jenny's question set her mind at rest about a certain Alvin Thomas, she hid it well. "God honors those who love and serve Him. Just make sure you never link your life with anyone who doesn't believe in Him."

"I won't," Jenny promised. A bright teary diamond hung on her lashes as she recalled at that moment the radiance in Laura's face at Don's homecoming.

Don had to leave Three Rivers on a Monday. Sunday after church he asked Laura to walk down to the river with him. He took her soft hand and led her on a worn path through shady woods. Suddenly he stopped. "Laura, I want to tell you something but I don't know how." He felt her tremble but she tightened her grip on his hand and he went on. "Laura, I love you with all of my heart. Will you marry me?"

Her happy tears fell in a bright waterfall. "I've loved you since the first time I saw you. Yes, Don, I'll marry you."

Don released her hand and picked a blade of grass. He bound it around her ring finger while the forest came alive with a symphony by songbirds sweeter than any wedding march. "This will have to do until I can get you a better ring," he told her. "I know now I always loved you, too, but I didn't realize it until I came home."

"I am so happy." Her clear eyes looked into his and Don gently kissed her for the first time and held her tightly in his arms. Easing herself from his grip, Laura said, "Let's go home and tell my folks, then go out and tell yours."

"I'll be surprised if they don't already know," Don teased.

"So will I." Laura's laughter bubbled over. "Especially Jenny."

On the long walk home they agreed that although they didn't want to postpone marriage, Don should remain with his year-round job. He would complete his tour of duty before their wedding. Their future life and happiness were forever rooted in Three Rivers, and that made their wedding worth the wait.

The Shipleys and Ashleys gave hearty approval and Jenny went into a transport of delight. "Now you'll be my real sister and not just my pretend one," she told Laura.

"That's part of the reason she's marrying me," Don couldn't help putting in, but the look in his eyes belied any such thing.

The next morning the Ashleys rose before

dawn. Don manfully told his parents goodbye at home, insisting he didn't want them waving him off from the little red depot. Jenny drove him to the station where Laura stood waiting on the platform. At first the three talked of trivial matters, with Jenny commenting on how Don's hearty breakfast would keep even his bottomless stomach sated until he reached the city. Then she casually sauntered away, leaving her brother and his brand-new fiancée alone amid the bustle of arrivals and departures.

The last of the baggage and mail sacks were loaded. The conductor bellowed, "All aboar-r-rd!" and Don held Laura close, kissed her, and tore free to leap to the bottom step of the rear coach as the train started to move. Two whistle blasts later, the Galloping Goose rounded a curve and vanished from sight.

In an effort to cheer Laura, Jenny persuaded her to go to Biddy Reed's for a famous cinnamon bun bursting with raisins and dripping with butter. "Don may have eaten a big breakfast, but I didn't," she confessed.

Laura agreed and soon they sat across from one another at a small table in the eating area of the rooming house. The usual breakfast crowd had long departed and gone to work and the nearly empty room offered privacy.

"Laura," Jenny began, "we're no longer children. We're young women and we need to start thinking about the future. You're going to marry Don but it won't be for a long time. I'm finished with school, I have no interest in college. I need to get a job to earn my living. It's not right for Mother and Father to continue supporting me." She paused to enjoy the roll and cold, sweet milk.

"One of us might clerk in the General Store or if Biddy needs help here, one of us could do that. But wouldn't you rather work together? I know you'll want to buy things to add to your hope chest. Things you can't make the way you do sheets and pillow slips and dishtowels."

"Oh, yes!" Laura perked up and her blue eyes shone. "But in Three Rivers isn't it going to be hard to get two jobs at the same place?" She wiped crumbs from her mouth.

Jenny shook her head. "Not as hard as you think. We could be flunkies in a logging camp."

Laura put down her milk glass. "Why, I never thought of that!"

"Remember when Alvin wanted to work in the woods but was too young for a rigging or cutting job? He really liked working in the cookhouse." She giggled. "For one thing, he could eat all he liked, and could he ever eat!"

"I know most of the camps hire boys," Laura said doubtfully. "But do they hire women?"

"Alvin says one or two of them do." Jenny cut another healthy slice of roll but let it dangle from her fork, intent on the conversation. "I love the outdoors and so do you. Besides, we will get paid a whole lot more than at any town job. We're free part of each day and the camps always want locals instead of outside help."

"Would it be ladylike? Mother and Dad will never consent if it isn't." Laura looked intrigued but Jenny could tell she wasn't convinced.

"I asked Alvin that exact question. He said the men respect women flunkies for the most part. In rare cases when a woman is insulted the camp superintendent immediately tells the offender to take his bedroll and hit the skids."

"Have you prayed about this, Jenny? I could never go work in a logging camp unless I knew the job wouldn't displease God." Laura lowered her voice.

"Both before and after I talked with

Alvin." Jenny leaned forward in her chair. "I even said something to him about it and his reply was that sometimes the women who serve as flunkies have a real chance to witness of Christ's love, simply by maintaining high standards and setting a good example. I think my parents will let me go, if yours will."

"I'll ask," her friend promised. "I'll give part of the money to help out at home and put the rest away." A vivid blush betrayed where Laura's thoughts had strayed, to a certain merchant marine on his final leg of duty.

Five

To Jenny and Laura's delight, one of the larger logging camps readily consented to take them on in flunky positions, but with a stipulation. "We can't use you for at least three weeks because we're shut down. The hot, dry weather gives us some time to get the equipment shipshape," the friendly camp superintendent told them. "Glad your folks agreed you can work for us, and I'll look forward to it."

"How will we ever get through the next weeks?" Jenny wondered aloud. "I love Three Rivers but life will be tiresome, I'm afraid." Except for the saloon fights, Three Rivers had always been a basically peaceful community.

Two days later she discovered how wrong she had been. During that afternoon Little Star rode out to the Ashleys when Laura was there.

"Why, Little Star! What's wrong?" Jenny stared with surprise at her usually calm friend. Little Star had slid off her Indian pony, run toward them and now appeared unable to speak. They led her inside where Andrew and Esther still sat at the dinner table.

"Child, what is it?"

Andrew Ashley's concerned voice seemed to embolden the young woman. "There's been a terrible killing," she stammered. Bit by bit the story came out. Doc Blanchard had been called east of town to a low plateau where a half-dozen families struggled to make a living on small ranches. Fertile ground needed water and only one small creek flowed through the area, provoking many quarrels over the use of the water. Those on the upper reaches always had plenty; ranchers downstream often had none. Yet the quarrels never developed beyond complaining.

Pete Borden's place lay at the extreme end of the settlement and he seldom had enough water for his stock. He claimed to have approached his neighbors again and again but they only laughed at his plight. Bitterness grew when his stock thirsted. Appeals to the law had been in vain.

On a morning fresh from the hand of God but marred by the devil's own hate, Borden loaded a rifle and started a shooting spree that ended with five dead. He then returned home and killed himself.

"It was so awful Doc Blanchard wouldn't let me go anywhere near," Little Star said with a sob. "I never saw him look so white and old. To make things worse, it happened across the county line. Their nearest law enforcement agency is fifty miles away at the county seat. Word had to be sent by telegraph from our railroad station. It will take twenty-four hours for the sheriff and deputies to get here. In the meantime, Doc's doing what has to be done and Daddy O'Toone's gone out to try and comfort the families who lost husbands, brothers, and fathers." She shook as if chilled.

Andrew slowly rose and crossed to the window. His wide shoulders slumped. "I've been afraid something unpleasant might happen, but not this."

"Why?" Jenny slipped to his side and put an arm around his waist.

"There have been rumors about a conspiracy to get rid of Borden and take his land. Ugly things. According to gossip, when he went to sell his hogs, no one would buy them. One man frankly said he'd been told the hogs died of cholera."

"That is horrible," Jenny cried.

"I know. I also heard certain men had

gone to the city where Pete Borden's fiancée lives and told her a bunch of vile lies. She believed them and broke the engagement."

Laura's face turned whiter than parchment. "How could anyone do such a thing?"

"No one will ever know the truth of the feud," Andrew predicted. "My guess is that Pete Borden stepped over the line of sanity, with terrible consequences." He turned back to Little Star. "I'm glad Doc didn't permit you to help this time."

"So am I. He told me to take the rest of the day off and I came here." She looked at her shaking hands. "Mr. Ashley, is it the curse of Eagle Feather? Is my grandfather to blame?"

Too shocked to speak, Jenny stood frozen to the floor. Esther Ashley said quietly, "Christians don't believe in Indian curses, Little Star. You know that."

Long-held superstition battled with Little Star's knowledge of the white man's God. Even though she had accepted Jesus Christ, at times her family's beliefs bound her like the strands of an invisible web. "I just don't know." She buried her face in her hands.

Jenny's heart nearly broke with compassion. How hard it was to be free of what you had been taught, even when Jesus came into your life bringing forgiveness and hope! Her thoughts turned uncontrollably to the curse Little Star had mentioned.

Chief Eagle Feather and his tribe originally inhabited the prairie, where they lived for years in the shadow of surrounding hills. Ample game and salmon provided food and fur for warm clothing. Then the white settlers came, armed with papers that said they owned the land.

Gathering his small band around him, legend has it he told them, "We must go from our home. I am old and weak. I do not know if I can start a life in the forest. Before I die, I vow that the white man will never succeed on the land he stole from Chief Eagle Feather and his people." The tribe slipped back into the forest, far away from the conquering white settlers for many years. During that time Chief Eagle Feather died and eventually his son Big Bear and younger braves cautiously made friends with a few white families and learned to trust them. They took jobs in the woods but consented to work only with their own people or one or two whites, such as Ben Shipley or Andrew Ashley.

Jenny was roused from her thoughts when her father spoke. "I know that particular prairie land has never been successful, Little

Star. There have been crop failures and disease among the animals but these things occur elsewhere as well. It's been wet and dry and locusts have attacked. Even so, your grandfather could have had no way of knowing all this. Some of the failures can be attributed to bad luck, others to mismanagement."

Little Star lifted a tear-stained face but didn't look convinced.

Andrew tried another tack. "You told me once Big Bear said Chief Eagle Feather never killed a single animal unless he needed food or the skin for shelter. Do you really think such a man would inflict a curse that brought death to men?"

A little color crept into Little Star's face and she slowly shook her head from side to side. Yet several hours later when she left them to ride back to town, Jenny watched her slump over her pony's back. "I wish we could help her."

"We can pray for her, right now." The four then knelt, joined hands, and prayed earnestly that the shock of the tragedy would not undermine the teachings of Daddy O'Toone. Neither Big Bear nor Little Star's mother White Cloud cared to hear about the white man's God. Furthermore, Jenny knew her Indian friend had always struggled with being different, ever since she had faced schoolchildren who refused to play with her years before.

"We stood by her then," Laura reminded when she and Jenny walked with Tammy to Pixie House after supper. "We'll stand by her now. There's sure to be a furor in Three Rivers and everyone will be dredging up that old Indian curse."

"I wish I could persuade her to stay out here for a few days until things settle down," Jenny said with a sigh. "It's the only thing I can think of but I don't think she'll come."

Her guess proved right. Little Star thanked Jenny but said she'd simply go on working with Doc. Yet she and Laura noticed how frightened she looked and how dull with worry her usually sparkling eyes had become.

The answer to their prayers came in an unexpected way. The three friends sang together in the church choir and always enjoyed Daddy O'Toone's sermons. Yet the one he preached the Sunday after the tragedy burned into their hearts. As he began to speak, his countenance glowed with the light of God. "We have lived through tragedy. So did God, when Jesus died on the cross. Today we must look up, not down, to our source of comfort and only hope of salvation. I have chosen as a topic, 'God's love for the mountains and wilderness.' " He opened his worn Bible and related the story told in Exodus 24 of how God commanded Moses to come to the mount. He went on to read other Scriptures of mountaintop and wilderness experiences. He shared his belief that God called people to the mountains and wilderness so they could commune with Him without distraction and interference. Light through a simple stained-glass window cast a rainbow arc on the tall, white-bearded minister and reminded the congregation of God's covenant with humankind.

The moment the service ended, Jenny whispered to Laura, "I know how to help Little Star!" Little gold flecks danced in her brown eyes. "Back me up." She herded Laura out and waited for Little Star to join them. "What do you say the three of us go on our own trip to the mountains, a real camping experience?"

"I'd love to," Laura promptly exclaimed.

"So would I." Little Star brightened, then the light in her face faded. "I don't know if I can get off work."

"We'll find out." Jenny hastened toward Doc Blanchard and the others followed. "Doc Blanchard, Laura and I want to go on a camping trip but it won't be half as much fun unless Little Star goes. May she?"

"Mother would be happy to help you while she's gone," Laura offered.

"She would, would she?" Bushy eyebrows met over the keen gray eyes. He turned to his assistant and Jenny could sense what he was thinking. *Too pale, too withdrawn. A trip will do her good.* "Go and have a wonderful time. Carrie Shipley's a crackerjack nurse and I'll be glad to have her."

When the gruff, kind-hearted doctor strolled away, Jenny offered her plan for the trip. "If we could get Big Bear to pack our supplies in and go with us, I've always wanted to see Glacier Peak and the high meadow country." Her friends seconded the suggestion.

A flurry of planning that lasted for three days began. Parents agreed to the idea; Aunt Carrie said she'd be glad to help Doc if needed. On Wednesday the three friends met at Biddy Reed's and Little Star reported that her father would not only take them, but pick up all needed supplies. "Just bring your own blankets and what clothes you need," she advised. The interest in her eyes was an unexpected reward for Jenny.

Early morning shadows still blanketed Three Rivers when Big Bear placed the last of their supplies on the pack animal. His deft hands formed a diamond hitch so the pack wouldn't shift, while Tammy danced around his feet until Jenny ordered her away. A last-minute drink from a nearby well and the quartet started out, with White Knight prancing and the other horses following his lead. Once out of town they began to sing all their favorite hymns but once into the forest, the group fell silent. Jenny listened first to the birds then heard the creak of saddle leather at each bend of the trail. At Cougar Hollow a four-point buck leaped gracefully across the trail. A red squirrel scolded from the branches of a Sitka spruce. Salmon berries, wild roses, and a waterfall brought exclamations of joy. Two otters across the river at Murphy's Bar gleefully took turns sliding down the slippery mud bank until Tammy's bark frightened them away.

Big Bear halted them at the confluence of the White Chuck and Sauk rivers. Lunch had never tasted so good. A few miles of dusty travel later, they crossed the Sauk on a cable suspension bridge that swayed spasmodically under the horses' hooves. Most people preferred to walk and lead their mounts across; the three friends were no exception and Jenny felt a bit dizzy when they reached the other side. After a brief rest they remounted and continued their journey.

From dense forest to a thicket of alder and vine maple saplings along the bank of a small pond they traveled. A loud splash brought them to a halt.

"Oh, look!" Jenny pointed to a well-constructed beaver dam and Little Star laughingly explained the splashing sound hadn't come from a large fish — Laura's idea — but from the beavers' paddlelike tails that warned of impending danger. Before they rode on Mama and Papa Beaver nonchalantly emerged from the water and went back to chewing on small alder trees already bearing their signatures.

Big Bear spent the time checking the horses and packs. Hours and miles in the saddle eventually took their toll. When they reached their first day's destination at the North Fork Bridge, they stretched and pitched in to set up camp. They fetched water and then moss for their beds; Big Bear cared for the riding ponies and unloaded the pack horse. A quick dip in the icy river left them more than ready for the string of native trout Big Bear caught and cleaned, then cooked over the open fire. Jenny and Laura marveled at the expert way their guide and Little Star boiled coffee in a bucket hung over the coals from a forked stick and flipped bannocks into the air to bake the other side.

Tall tales and singing dwindled into sleep as the long day ended. The next morning bacon, eggs, and flapjacks greeted them.

"Big Bear, you should hire out to do this," Jenny said with her mouth full.

He shook his head. "Too many come but would not see." Jenny tucked the thought away to take out and consider later.

"Let's go off the main trail leading to White Pass and Glacier Lake so we can see some other country," Little Star suggested. The others endorsed her suggestion and when they saw the sapphire Goat Lake, partially encircled by a centuries-old glacier, no one regretted the side trip. Neither did they begrudge a two-hour ride to Round Lake at about 4,500 feet. The lake wasn't outstanding but they were quick to marvel at the mule deer, black bears, and mountain goats. Sloan Peak, Bedal Peak, and Pinnacle Peak with its crows'-nest defied description.

"What a wonderful place to spend a summer," Jenny exclaimed, staring at the crows'-nest then at majestic Glacier Peak in the distance, snow-capped and beckoning.

"Father used to hunt mountain goat for

meat and for the wool Mother makes into warm sweaters and stockings," Little Star told them.

Big Bear added tales of Canadian Indians who came across the border and stole small boys from his tribe; of a lake where one must never fire a gun or throw a rock for fear of a violent storm; of trapping the wolverine, marten, and cougar for pelts.

Jenny carefully refrained from looking at her companions. She might not believe stories sacred to the Indian people but she had been taught to show respect by courteously listening without commenting.

Eventually they reached the base of White Pass. Nineteen switchbacks brought them to the summit of White Mountain at 6,000 feet and in the heart of alpine meadows. Laura counted eleven separate mountain ridges, one behind the other. Two miles more around the side of the hill and the weary riders stopped in awe. Silhouetted against the clear blue sky in all her pristine beauty stood her majesty, Glacier Peak.

After a long period of silence, Jenny quoted, " 'The heavens declare the glory of God; and the firmament sheweth his handywork.' "*

*Psalm 19:1 (KJV)

Laura added in a soft whisper, " 'The fool hath said in his heart, There is no God.' "*

"How can anyone doubt the existence of God after this?" Jenny added. She impulsively turned to Big Bear. He sat motionless in the saddle, as if dreaming. Then he pointed to the snow-draped monarch and spoke to Little Star.

"My daughter, when Great Spirit calls, we come here again to join our people."

"Yes, Father." She turned pleading eyes toward Jenny, who nodded. She and Jenny knew it made little difference where one's body lay. The important thing was knowing Jesus and living in the expectation of His return.

Please, Father, Jenny silently prayed, *let Little Star's parents and tribe one day know Your Son.*

All too soon the time and the scenery flowed past. Cinder Mountain. Meander Meadows, saved until last because of its beauty. The dramatic cliffs with their ever-changing splashes of color from the setting sun and granite peaks with their curious shadows and white aprons of snow were typical vistas. Jenny would never forget the thunder of a distant avalanche or the nearby

*Psalm 53:1 (KJV)

deer and ptarmigans, strange birds whose feathered feet turned white in winter. All these memories Jenny stored in the treasure chest of her mind, to be cherished in the future.

Meander Meadows burst upon them with its potpourri of fragrances from a hundred varieties of flowers, known and unknown. Rare avalanche lilies poked their six white petals through patches of snow. At lunch a bird Little Star identified as a camp robber or whiskey jack snatched Jenny's sandwich as she raised it to her mouth!

"Mount up now." Big Bear's commanding voice propelled them to their saddles. The guide handed a growling Tammy to Jenny and started them back down the trail, promising to follow. *Strange,* Jenny thought. *He always leads and Tammy hardly ever growls.*

"What is it?" Little Star asked her father but he didn't reply until they had traveled some distance.

"Pull up," he ordered. They stopped. Laura gasped and Jenny felt the hair on the back of Tammy's neck rise. "Quiet," she told her. A monstrous white bear lumbered out of a clump of trees, went about eating blueberries, then reared on its hind legs.

"He's caught our scent but isn't sure

where we are," Big Bear quickly told the frightened young women in an almost inaudible whisper. "Don't speak. A bear has poor eyesight, keen hearing." They retreated, leaving the bear to his feasting.

"Were you as scared as I?" Jenny asked after supper.

"Yes!" Laura said. She shivered and hunched closer to the campfire.

"Little Star?"

"I felt strange but knew Father would protect us. He isn't afraid of anything in the forest," she proudly boasted.

"I never saw a white bear," her father replied. "It must have weighed 800 pounds. Three Rivers people will laugh and say no white bear lives in forest but we know."

Kennedy Hot Springs offered their last camp and a chance to wash in plenty of hot water. The scream of a cougar interrupted their campfire chat but the echoes died in the distance.

At that moment Jenny experienced the same feeling she had on the train coming back to Three Rivers. Once again she felt she was between worlds for a time. Part of her wanted to stay longer in God's creation, a world of wonders no human would ever equal. Yet ahead lay more new experiences, working with Laura as a flunky, for one.

She let her gaze travel from Big Bear, who had become even bigger in her estimation, to Laura, who looked rosier and more vital than she had all summer.

Last she turned toward Little Star. The shadow of tragedy in her eyes had fled. Her mouth and eyes laughed at something Laura had said. She, too, appeared ready to leave the wilderness and go back to daily duty.

I wonder if Jesus sometimes felt this way, Jenny mused. *When duty called Him from time apart with His Father, did He look both forward and back? I think if He were here to-night, He might. . . .* She fell asleep in the middle of her sentence. The next afternoon the travelers returned to Three Rivers.

Six

Keith stood at the window of his Pinnacle Peak crows'-nest and watched the boiling clouds race toward each other, blend, and sweep on. All the days of beauty and nights of grandeur could not compare with the scowling sky on all four sides of him. Zigzags of white lightning split the grayness in two. Thunder reverberated between the peaks. "I'm in for it," Keith said. Yet he couldn't tear his fascinated gaze away from the oncoming storm, even when he saw balls of light from static electricity roll along the mountainside. He waited until a weird blue light danced all around the lookout then raced to his insulated glass chair. Nothing could hurt him while he stayed in it.

"Just like You, God. As long as we stay in Your will, we'll be safe and protected."

The Fourth of July fireworks he had just witnessed couldn't hold a roman candle to this exhibition, Keith thought with a chuckle. As larger light balls skimmed the ridges and hills like ghostly apparitions, the wind made a shrieking sound as if a thousand devils had been loosed from captivity. The storm raged for another half-hour before moving on to distant peaks. Keith left his glass chair and watched it go. Perhaps never in his life had he felt so invigorated, so aware of the power of God. "If it is Your will," he prayed, "I can be happy the rest of my life here near Three Rivers."

The heavens split and wept, a cloudburst that brought relief. The storm would have set a myriad of fires were it not for the squall that left as suddenly as it had come.

The next morning Keith carefully checked with his binoculars but not a wisp of smoke drifted up to announce live embers. Bushes and stunted trees below him glistened like diamonds in the brilliant sun. A cloud or two sailed by, as if to remind the man who dared live in a crows'-nest that the spectacle of last night might have a repeat performance.

Day after day Keith worked, dreamed, and drank his fill of his surroundings. One day when his duties permitted he took pencil and paper and began to write. Sometimes as a child he had scribbled little poems but this one came from a mature heart.

God's Country

Give me a home in the wildwood
On the banks of a silvery stream
Where all is peaceful and quiet,
Where living is like a dream.

Where the forest remains primeval,
Void of disfigurement or mar.
Where no man yet has ventured
To etch his ugly scars.

Where the columbine and jonquil
Bloom 'round my cabin door,
Where flows the sweet spring water
Across the valley floor.

Where the coyotes howl at midnight
And the woodcock wakes me at
    dawn,
Where I find the friendly beaver
And the newborn, spotted fawn.

Give me a home in the mountains
Where the wildflowers bloom every
    year,
Where the birds forever sing gaily
For they know not the meaning of
    fear.

Where at dusk I hear the rustling
Of the golden aspen's leaves,
Like shiny pennies from heaven
Falling gently down through the
　　trees.

Where the mallards and the
　　pintails
Are on the wing once more,
Searching for a nesting place
Somewhere along the shore.

Here I'll have time to be thankful
For all the things I see,
Here I know I will realize
Your best gifts are always free.

Give me a home in the high lands
Where the treetops touch the sky,
Give me a home in Your country,
　　God,
　To serve You until I die.

Keith laid down his pencil, his heart
bursting. He realized then that he had not
written a poem but a prayer. He carefully
folded the page and tucked it away in his
Bible. Perhaps someday he would show it to
Jennifer Ashley. He had a feeling that she of
all people would understand. . . .

★ ★ ★

In spite of Jenny's wish to the contrary, many changes began to take place in and around Three Rivers. Horse logging — over skid roads constructed of small, well-greased logs or poles placed crosswise eight feet apart — gave way to high-speed steam donkeys capable of yarding, or delivering, thirty or more railroad flatcar log loads per day. Powerfully geared locomotives, the Shay and Heisler, negotiated the steep mountain grades. The old link and pin system that had connected the flatcars was replaced with individual air brake systems, resulting in greater efficiency and a higher standard of safety.

New families arrived in Three Rivers to work in the camps. Most came from the South, especially North Carolina and Tennessee. Once a newcomer liked the area, he sent for friends and relatives. Some were experienced woodsmen, others were not. Andrew Ashley had helped carry a dozen of these injured newcomers out of the woods, often down slopes so steep only the loggers' cork, or calk, boots with their nail-sharp calks kept them from sliding on needle-covered terrain. Doc Blanchard patched the wounded loggers up and usually in a few weeks they returned to work. The most feared job hazard, however, was dead snags, or widowmakers. If a falling tree hit a snag, it could course.

Laura and Jenny had watched the mountain storm with excitement, especially when the rains came. They would be able to start their flunky jobs a few days earlier than expected. One of the camps that hired over a hundred men also accepted women and welcomed the extra hands. A significant part of their job would be setting tables, a task they had performed countless times at home. Haying at the Ashleys and Shipleys meant as much work for the women as the men. Neighbors methodically went from one place to another and the girls and women cooked, set tables, and served the large, hungry crews.

Such logging job titles as chasers, chokermen, and donkey punchers were unfamiliar to Jenny and Laura. Jenny's first embarrassing predicament on her new job was a result of her ignorance. She didn't hear a new man ask a seasoned logger what his job was. She only heard the reply, "I'm choking."

Jenny set down the enormous dishes of hot food with a little crash and pounded the big logger on the back.

He coughed, then looked bewildered and

asked, "What are you doing, lassie?" His blue eyes twinkled.

"I-I heard you say you were choking!" She stared at him, realized he was perfectly all right, and wished she could fall through the floor when the dining room resounded with laughter at her expense. Then she ran for the kitchen, her hands over her ears.

The big Irishman followed her. "Forget it," he advised, standing in the doorway. He turned and pointed at the watching men. "If any of you guys give her trouble, I'll choke *you!*"

The laughter died and Jenny bravely took up her duties but avoided looking at the men until they went back to eating and pretended to ignore her.

One day Laura took Jenny aside while they were waiting to serve a huge breakfast. "You know, it's funny. We've been raised in a lumber town but never before saw the inner workings of a modern camp like this. Look at that cook stove." She pointed at the huge stove with its three large ovens.

"And the pots and pans and ladles over the dish-up tables," Jenny added. "It's still incredible on how large a scale things are done. Three cooks to make hotcakes." She gestured at the assembly line of the cooks. One busily poured batter onto a gigantic grill. The second followed and turned the cakes while the third had his hands more than full simply flipping the piping hot cakes onto platters so the women could rush them to the tables.

"This camp hires the best cooks they can get," Laura confided. "I'm glad we got jobs here. I like Kate and Maude too." The older women had been so helpful that the new flunkies had quickly caught on to their duties.

"It's nice the way our schedule goes, too," Laura said. While some of the Three Rivers men went home nights in a crummy or mulligan car provided by the company, most stayed in camp and went to town for the weekends, lessening the work. This gave the friends every other weekend off, and the opportunity they both relished to attend church. On those treasured days Jenny also spent time with Alvin, and Laura wrote extra long letters to Don.

In time the loggers and the flunkies became friends. They laughed and joked together but always the men treated the young women with respect. Jenny felt especially close to those who consistently sat at "her" table. When the dreaded seven whistle blasts from one of the donkeys signaled someone had been hurt, her busy hands would still as she said a whispered prayer. Would it be one of her good friends? Three whistles called for the locomotive and the other four summoned the Bull of the Woods (the boss). Only once did a man lose his life during her tour of duty. Broken arms and legs and saw and axe cuts accounted for the other accidents.

The logging camp had its lighter side that surfaced frequently. One day an obnoxious character not long in the camp violated the unwritten but inflexible law of not bothering the flunkies. Kate, a buxom girl not likely to win any beauty contests but an excellent worker with high moral character, was busy serving her supper table. As she was about to deposit the evening's entrée on the table, an odd-looking man with a head as bald as a billiard ball reached out and pinched her leg.

"You bum!" Kate's eyes flashed with fury. She deliberately turned the enormous bowl of hot spaghetti and tomato sauce on top of his shiny head.

"Ow!" As he leaped up, trying to rid himself of his misplaced dinner, the entire dining room howled with laughter. The most ferocious beast in the forest couldn't equal the ghastly sight of two eyes staring grotesquely through a wig of soggy spaghetti and red sauce dripping from his ears.

"What's carrying on in here?" Big Jim Callihan, the Irishman Jenny had pounded, marched over, grabbed the drenched man by the nape of the neck, and carried him to the wide open door. "Pick up your time and git," he ordered, then gave the offender a mighty shove that sent him sprawling onto the board porch. "An' don't try to get a job with any of the other camps around here, Meatball. There's no place for the likes of you."

"And good riddance!" Kate called as she went to the kitchen for more spaghetti. "Meatball" vanished from the ranks but the story and his new name ran rampant throughout Three Rivers and Kate received much support and praise.

Summer passed quickly. An autumn chill now tinged the nights and early mornings. Head ranger Matt Davis had already sent word for his lookout men to vacate their crows'-nests and return to town. Before long snow would crown the surrounding hills.

Keith Burgess was first to leave his post. He had much to do and a lingering sense of regret filled him all the time he closed his station. After a late start off Pinnacle Peak he decided to stop by a logging camp and spend the night. Anyone passing was always welcome to meals and a night's lodging for a small fee. The loggers were seated first in their regular places and then visitors took the empty seats. As Keith surveyed the long room, all the while sniffing the hearty, onion-laced stew, he froze.

Was his imagination playing tricks on him? The young woman in a simple pink dress who stepped forward to show him to the table looked more beautiful than he remembered her. What on earth was Jennifer Ashley doing *here?* He rubbed his eyes, swept the room with a glance, and saw a blue-gowned girl he recognized as Laura Shipley.

"Right this way, please."

An hour earlier Keith had been ravenous. Now all he wanted to do was sit and stare at the woman he had dreamed about all summer.

Passing Laura in the kitchen doorway, Jenny had a chance to whisper, "Goodness, did you see who just seated himself at my table?"

"How could I miss him? He's the best-looking man I've seen in ages." Laura cast a roguish glance at Jenny. "If it weren't for Don, I'd wish the visitor were at *my* table."

Jenny inconspicuously stole glances at the

tall, good-looking fellow as much as her serving duties permitted. Strange, she had never seen him before yet the same beating of her heart that came when she was away from Alvin — but never when she was with him — made her wonder at herself. She saw Kate and Maude casting envious glances her way and secretly rejoiced.

Keith took as much time eating as he dared and didn't leave until the last logger rose and started out. The flunkies had already begun clearing tables while Jenny stood putting fruit on a table near the door. Many of the loggers liked taking fruit to the bunkhouse for a bedtime snack. Keith tried to think of something to say when he passed Jenny that wouldn't sound audacious. His temples throbbed and he could feel blood racing through his veins. Just before he got to her, he blurted out, "You sure can ride a horse!"

"Why, how did you know?" If Jenny thought the remark ridiculous, she didn't show it. Rich color swept into her face.

"I saw you at the Fourth of July race."

"Oh." Jenny looked down at the fruit. "Would you like an orange for the bunk-house? I mean, for a snack in the bunk-house?" She laughed and broke the tension.

Quiet Laura, who could still be a cutup,

casually walked by and in a saucy tone said, "Why don't you take the man's hat and ask him in, Jenny?"

She turned rosy. "I-I have to get on with my work." She shot a just-wait-until-I-get-you-alone look at her friend.

"Miss Ashley, would you walk with me when you finish?"

Jenny took in his honest eyes and the respectful admiration in his face. In a low voice she said, "Perhaps, but just for a short time. I don't think I know your name."

"Keith Burgess." He inclined his head then went out.

Jenny hurried to remove the rest of the dirty dishes and get her table set for breakfast.

"Are you mad at me?" Laura grinned at her.

"Not mad, but maybe annoyed. If you'll help me finish I'll forgive you. I want to get through quickly."

"Don't tell me you're going to see him again tonight!" Laura stood stockstill, her mouth open.

"Just for a little while." Jenny spoke the truth. Nine o'clock meant lights out for everyone.

The only place nearby that offered a modicum of privacy lay beside the shining railroad tracks. They sauntered along in the early evening, with lengthening shadows beginning to fall.

"Are you a new employee here?" she asked.

"No, I'm working to become a forest ranger." Keith threw back his curly blond head and breathed deeply.

Before he could add that he had been a lookout firewatcher she said, "It's strange that I didn't see you in Three Rivers."

"I only spent a day or two and one of them was the Fourth of July. I have the necessary education to be a ranger but I'm going to take some courses in timber management and sales. I'll be gone this winter to attend school."

"Oh." Her response sounded flat in the clear air.

"Would it be all right if I stop by to see you the next time I pass by?" he asked.

"Yes." Jenny turned back toward the way they had come. "We must go back now."

"I know." He silently walked her to the steps of the quarters she shared with the other three flunkies. "Goodbye for now, Miss Ashley."

"Goodbye, Mr. Burgess." She held out her slim hand and he engulfed it in his.

The moment he reached the bunkhouse and got out of earshot, Laura, Maude, and

Kate, who Jenny had seen peeping out, started teasing unmercifully.

" 'Goodbye *for now*, Miss Ashley,' " Maude mimicked. "Don't forget I said *for now*."

Laura's laugh pealed out. "He's smitten, Jenny. Absolutely smitten." Her pretty face could not conceal her mirth. "The very first time he sees you this perfect stranger falls in love with you."

Jenny could only inanely retort, "It isn't the first time."

"What? Have you been holding out on us?" the unmerciful trio demanded. "When did you meet him before?"

"I didn't." Jenny modestly undressed beneath her full dress so she could slip into a warm flannel gown.

"You're exasperating, Jennifer Ashley," Kate accused, yet her round face held no malice. "If it isn't the first time he saw you then how can you have just met?"

Her voice muffled by the thick cloth folds, Jenny took refuge for an instant. "He saw me ride on the Fourth of July but I didn't see him." She pulled the gown down and her dress off.

"So it could still have been love at first sight." Laura's eyes danced. " 'Romeo, oh, Romeo . . .' "

Her Shakespearean quote broke off when the pillow Jenny fired hit her dead center.

"Nine o'clock, girls," Kate reminded from her bed. "Time enough tomorrow to tease Jenny." She turned and soon her even breathing showed she slept.

But Laura surprised her friend by slipping to Jenny's bed in the dark and giving her a quick hug before whispering, "He's a Christian. I noticed that before he ate, he pretended to drop his napkin but his eyes were closed and his lips moved." For the life of her, Jenny couldn't figure out why she felt so glad.

Seven

Keith left the next morning shortly after breakfast for his long walk to Three Rivers, unable to think up an excuse to linger in camp. Besides, Jenny wouldn't be able to talk with him. She had her work to do. He sighed when he thought that for the second time he was leaving her behind.

He had almost reached town where he would report in to Matt Davis before catching the Galloping Goose when someone hollered, "Hey, Burgess!" Pounding hooves skidded to a stop and a laughing voice demanded, "Through with the lookout for the year?"

"Now that fall's here, I have to get back to my studies." Keith recognized the three young men who had ridden up as the Brice brothers. True outdoorsmen, they had ridden in the Pinnacle Peak area during the summer.

"I sure like autumn," Bill, the oldest of the three, exclaimed. "Just look at that." He waved toward frosted vine maples, splashing crimson and yellow against falling golden aspen leaves. Feathered plumes of blood-red sumac stood tall. Golden pumpkins adorned a nearby field and ragged corn stalks awaited cutting.

"It's beautiful, but it's sad," Keith agreed.

A keen look of understanding flashed between him and Bill as Bob Brice said, "We can always look forward to the bluebirds, thrushes, and swallows coming back in the spring. Those, too." He pointed to a great V-shaped flock of wild geese winging their way south. "Ma and the girls are filling the root cellars with their canning. We've been cutting wood but now we're free for a few days and we're going hunting."

A thrill swept through Keith. Over the years he had been just too busy to get in much recreation. "You have a wonderful time to go."

Bill shot a quick glance at his brothers before he casually said, "Want to go with us? You don't have to leave Three Rivers today, do you?"

Keith's heart leaped. "Not really. I have to report in to Matt Davis and . . ."

"We'll wait for you. Bob and Ed and I were just going in for supplies. Plenty of

time. We're going up to Green Mountain."
Bill frowned. "These years are lean and we
need a good supply of meat for winter. Pa
butchered a couple of hogs and a steer but
venison can go a long way."

Keith wasted little time in making his
report and rejoining the Brices. To his con-
sternation, Bill and Ed stood glaring at a
hapless Bob who had awkwardly slipped
from the board sidewalk and sat on its edge
holding his ankle. "What's wrong?"

"Clumsy oaf went and sprained his foot,"
Ed said disgustedly.

"Does that mean the trip's off?"

"No-o-o." Bill cocked his head and his
bright blue eyes surveyed Keith and Ed.
"Doc will fix Bob up and get him home. The
three of us can still go. Sorry, brother, you
miss out this time."

Bob managed a shaky grin. "Well, since I
can't ride with this confounded foot, let
Keith take my horse. He's a good one and
fresh."

"Thanks, Brice." Keith mounted and followed Bill and Ed out of town. Miles lay between them and their destination and there
was no time to loiter.

"A fellow can't help but be glad to be alive
in such a world," Keith burst out as they
rode on rough logging roads through the

golden world of whirling leaves toward the Suiattle country. A few miles from where they wanted to cross the Sauk River a settler had a cabin. The Brices had arranged with him to take their supplies over in his rowboat while the riders swam their horses. Keith again thrilled to the adventure that lay ahead. Even the steady downpour that began before they reached their chosen campsite couldn't dampen his spirits, or the Brices'. Bill and Ed were experienced woodsmen and soon had a good shelter of cedar boughs standing. Getting wet meant little in their lives and the hot fire quickly dried all their clothes.

"The rain will probably stop soon," Ed hoped out loud.

Keith didn't mind one bit just staying in their cozy camp and getting better acquainted with his companions. Bill somehow kept the campfire burning, and the coffee perking, in the downpour. Yet when the torrent continued for hours, amid terrifying thunder rumbles that reverberated between the towering granite peaks around them, Keith shivered. To kill time, the Brices told humorous tales and offered bits of woodslore.

The rain continued the second day and then the third, and their formerly jovial

115

spirits were considerably dampened. Food supplies ran low. They had only planned to stay three days. The fourth morning the rain let up. Bill set his jaw and ordered, "Saddle up. It's fifteen miles back to where we cross the river and we don't know what we'll find."

Hungry and dispirited at the outcome of the trip that had seemed so promising, Keith and Ed followed Bill on his commanding black horse Dynamite. Yet neither complained. Keith hunched down farther into Bob's slicker as rivulets of water dripped off his nose. *It will make a good story someday,* he wryly thought. But the sight that greeted him when they reached the river froze him to the saddle.

Where had the friendly Sauk gone? Usually tranquil, now a surging mass of mud and debris dirtied a wall of water. Logs, stumps, and even whole uprooted trees pitched and tossed on the crest of the river like matchsticks.

"Too late today to do anything," Bill muttered. "We'll pitch in, build some kind of shelter and a fire. Tomorrow we'll see."

Keith marveled at the young man. He had learned that Bill was only eighteen, but the forester made no effort to take charge because of his added years. This young man of the woods knew more than most old timers, and it showed in every move he made.

The trio slept little and rose at daybreak. Ed concocted, in his words, "a reasonable imitation of minute pudding" from their almost nonexistent supplies: a little flour, a bit of sugar, and a can of condensed milk. "We're so hungry anything will taste good," he said hopefully as he cooked the pudding over the fire.

Keith took a bite and choked but managed to swallow it. So did Ed. Bill put a spoonful in his mouth and immediately headed for the brush to spit it out.

"That's it." He set his firm lips in a grim line. "I'm going for help." He strode to Dynamite and saddled him.

"In *that?*" Ed pointed to the swollen river that had increased its roar in the night. "You're crazy, Bill Brice, absolutely crazy." He squared off and glared at his brother but Keith saw the shine of tears in the younger boy's eyes. "Just 'cause you're the oldest and told the folks you'd take care of us doesn't mean I'm going to let you commit suicide out there. Look!" He jabbed a thumb toward the river. Another monstrous tree complete with tearing, trailing roots thicker than a man's wrist swept past, crashed against the opposite shore, and bounced back with the shriek of an avalanche.

"I promised. We have no choice. There are no houses on this side of the river and we don't have a chance of getting a deer in this weather, you know that as well as I do." His voice cracked like a pistol.

"Then we'll all go," Keith put in, although his heart beat with terror at the very idea.

"You and Ed will stay here and wait for me," Bill snapped. "Think I can keep my mind on getting across the river if I have to worry about you two?"

Ed dug his toe in the muddy ground and mumbled, "Why don't we just hunker down until someone comes?"

"Grow up, Ed. The folks don't know how much food we packed. They won't even worry for days. We didn't say when we'd be back."

"I could make another minute pudding." Ed's feeble joke brought a look of disgust from Bill and then his usual happy smile lighted up his tanned face.

"I'd as lief face the river as eat that stuff. Hey, Dynamite's the best. He will get me there." He double-checked the cinches, tightened the girth a bit more, and swung easily into the saddle.

"Isn't there anything we can do?" Keith

118

helplessly asked, wondering that the words could get past the lump in his throat at the young woodsman's gallantry and bravery.

"You can pray." Bill's blue eyes softened. "The Almighty's been powerful good to our family and my ma and pa have always taught us He's there when we need Him. He cares for His own."

Keith sensed how hard it was for Bill to speak aloud the faith he possessed in abundance. He silently gripped the steady hand that Bill held out and saw Ed throw back his head and do the same.

"Don't worry." Bill swerved Dynamite a little to one side and started down the slippery bank then dug his heels into his horse's sides. "Let her rip, old boy!"

After the first terrified leap into the dark, swirling water, Dynamite's tired muscles responded and he swam in spite of the diabolical river. Ed and Keith stood tense and watching. "In flood time, the river's a lot higher in the middle than at the edges," the boy explained, his hands clenched.

Keith felt his own nails bite into his palms and gulped when a large windfall of trees and debris rushed sidewise downstream directly toward Dynamite and Bill. "Dear God, help them!" His involuntary cry rang above the storm.

"Ride, Bill!" Ed screamed.

The turbulent water became a swirling eddy. For a few seconds it caught the windfall in its circling motion, giving the two in its path time to forge ahead. They had reached the halfway point and disappeared behind a great wave. Were they lost, sucked under by the giant swell? Keith strained his eyes and prayed, aware of Ed sobbing beside him.

"Dear God, thank You!" Ed clenched Keith's arm with a grip of iron. The rolling waves had spewed horse and rider from their depths, soaked but alive. Bill hunched over Dynamite's neck and another wild torrent caught and swept them downstream a hundred yards. Keith stared at a wide sandbar a half-mile below. Would the current carry and deposit them there? He lost sight of them again. "We shouldn't have let him go."

"We couldn't have stopped him." Ed's fingers dug even deeper into Keith's arm. "When Bill makes up his mind something is right, nothing on earth will keep him from doing it. I just hope I can someday be half the man he is."

"You don't think he's gone for good?" Keith yanked his arm free and stared at the hated river.

"I guess God didn't help him." Ed's voice sounded hollow.

"*Wait*. Look, Ed, look!" A half-mile downriver a tired-looking horse carrying a sodden crouched figure stumbled onto the shore and stood, sides heaving. What felt like an eternity later Bill straightened, clasped both hands over his head, and then pointed to the sky and he and his valorous horse disappeared into a cottonwood thicket.

Silenced by the magnificent fight, Keith and Ed stood without speaking for a long time. Then Ed said, "He still has miles to go to reach the settler's cabin and he's weak."

Keith turned on him fiercely. "Man, do you think God would get them through the river and not give strength to finish the job?"

Ed flushed then held out a hand. "Burgess, I'm glad you're here."

"So am I, but if you'd asked me that a few minutes ago I'm not sure I could have said so," Keith admitted honestly. "Let's get a fire going. We still have to wait." A new thought struck him. "S'pose the settler won't bring the boat?"

"He'll bring it. My brother will see to that."

Hours later, after a boat ride Keith hoped

never again to duplicate, the burly, white-faced man confirmed Ed's prediction. "Bill come bustin' in demandin' I come git you fellers an' I told him he was insane." He scratched his head and wrung water from his beard. "He just up an' says, 'My brother and friend are over there starving. We're going.' Somethin' in his eyes made me stop arguin'. I sent my boy fer Bill's dad. My boat's a six-passenger an' I knew it'd take all three of us to git across." He shoved a heavy forelock back and grinned sheepishly. "I still ain't too sartain why I come."

"We're glad you did," Keith told him, but when he started to thank Bill, the exhausted hero brushed it off.

"Forget it. I got you into it; it was up to me to get you out. I'll come back for Bob and Ed's horses when the water goes down."

"Want some minute pudding?" Ed teased.

"Another crack like that and I'll pitch you back in the river," Bill told his rapidly recovering brother, who obligingly dumped the mixture on the fire, doused it, and grinned.

Soft-spoken Bill could also tease. When he rode into Three Rivers the next day with Keith, who had gladly accepted the invitation to spend the night at the Brice ranch, he said, "Don't s'pose you'll want to go on another hunting trip with us, will you?"

Keith's blue eyes sparkled as much as Bill's. He carefully mimicked, "Don't s'pose I don't want to, do you?" His laughter died. "It will have to be another year, though. Schoolbells are ringing for me right now."

"You're a real pard, Burgess." A lean, brown hand shot out. "I don't take many men hunting. They complain and make life miserable. You can go with the Brice boys any time you want."

Although Keith didn't get to see Jenny again before he left, his heart felt warm and light at the implied praise in Bill Brice's farewell.

The coming of the steam donkey brought new life and prosperity to Three Rivers. Automobiles arrived on the scene: a half-dozen or more Model T Fords; one Chalmers; one Oldsmobile; and the camp superintendent drove a Winton Six with fancy wire wheels. The road from Three Rivers to the nearest town received improvements and an enterprising man established jitney service. The thirty-mile trip took four hours in dry weather, six or more in rain or snow. The jitney sometimes got stuck in chuck holes or had flat tires. If it got mired in a deep rut, the driver simply walked to the nearest ranch and hired a team of horses to pull it free. Keeping the windshield clear also posed a problem, as the wiper had to be operated by hand from inside the vehicle. The driver proceeded in snowy weather, driving with one hand and operating the wiper with the other.

The first time an auto came to Three Rivers, it caused such a sensation small boys chased it around town. When it stopped, they peered underneath to find the horses that made the contraption go. One farmer had his horse and wagon tied to a hitching post while he bought groceries. A new auto rounded a corner and the frightened horse lunged, snapped his tethering rope, and headed for home. Doc Blanchard saw the runaway and grabbed the bridle. To the horse, Doc's "Whoa, boy, whoa" might as well have been "Good morning." When the horse reached a barn wearing little more than the bridle — the wagon had been severed long before — the incident did not amuse either the owner or residents who had been forced to run for their lives.

Jenny's family was not from North Carolina but she loved the Tarheels who came to Three Rivers. Some found them clannish because they minded their own business and expected others to do the same. To Jenny, once they accepted you as a friend, you had warm defenders for life. Some came from the mountains but those who called them hillbillies earned their scorn.

Jenny often visited the Brices who always insisted that she stay for supper. She liked their soft drawl and hospitality, especially when they said "y'all stay for supper," "ah reckon so," and "over yon." When she would ask one of the Brices how he was, he invariably would say "tol'ably well" or "ailin' bad."

Little Star discovered the same thing on her rounds with Doc Blanchard. At first her black eyes opened wide at the foreign-sounding speech but after a few months, she had picked it up and spoke more like a Tarheel than a native Indian. The town benefited from the southern culture as evidenced by square dances and "play parties," good old mountain music played by banjo, fiddle, guitar, and sometimes a jug that someone blew into.

Ever since Jenny had visited Glacier Peak, she had considered something even more daring than riding in the Fourth of July race. She wanted to write a book. No one in

Three Rivers had ever aspired to such an endeavor, but she had little time to make it a reality. One weekend while visiting home an idea came that offered a solution. "Is it another of my crazy ideas?" she prayed. "It would take a strong commitment." The more she thought about it, the more she felt convinced she should explore the idea.

Midmorning on a clear, cold day, she threw a saddle on White Knight and rode into town. A woman with a purpose, she trotted past Jake Lieberman's General Store and Biddy Reed's rooming house with its mouth-watering odors. She headed straight for the ranger station and found Matt Davis at his desk compiling seasonal reports.

Large, broad-shouldered, and well over six feet, when he courteously stood, his size alone was enough to frighten Jenny. What would he say when she told him why she'd come?

"What a nice surprise. I don't have many beautiful young women visit me."

Jenny felt as out of place as a schoolchild in a university. She knew if she didn't respond immediately, she'd never have the courage to speak at all. With a quick, silent prayer, she threw back her shoulders, looked straight into his weathered face, and blurted out, "I would like to work as a lookout in one of your crows'-nests."

Matt Davis's jaw dropped. Then he roared with laughter. "You're joking. No woman has ever been hired as a firewatcher, at least not to my knowledge."

"Does that matter?" Smarting under his reaction, Jenny persisted. "Is there any reason a woman couldn't do the job? Not on Pinnacle Peak or Liberty Bell, of course." She flashed a smile and hope stirred when she saw the thoughtful look that crept into his eyes. "They're too rugged even for me! On the other hand, Flower Dome is a lot lower and more easily accessible."

Matt's laughter turned to a smile of admiration. "It's a lonely life, Jenny. Not many folks visit the crows'-nests."

"I wouldn't mind." She pressed the point and eagerness spilled into her voice. "I'd enjoy it and I know about the woods." She didn't add, *and it would give me time to write.*

"I do need a lookout on Flower Dome next year," he admitted. "I'm willing to give you a try if you really want the job and feel you can handle it."

"I do."

"By gum, I believe you can." He clasped his hands behind his head. "You've convinced me. I'll notify you in the spring when to report for duty."

"Thank you, Mr. Davis." Jenny wanted to run and shout and thank God for her good fortune but she demurely shook hands with her new boss and left. Yet once in the street she raced to White Knight and pelted down Main Street and out toward the Shipley home. Wouldn't Laura be surprised when she heard the news!

Eight

With the coming of winter the logging camp shut down and Jenny and Laura returned home. Already nearby ponds and lakes had frozen into a shiningly transparent black ice that enticed all ages to don skates and show their skill. Two places in the lake closest to Three Rivers never froze because of warm water springs near the edges. Barn lanterns placed near these spots warned skaters of the danger.

Once a young man who had come to town the previous spring didn't know the reason for the lanterns. He decided to use one to look for more wood for the warming fire that shot flames high into the crisp night sky. He skated around the edge of the lake at high speed, unnoticed by the others, picked up the lantern, and then *splash!* He plunged headlong into the icy water. Fortunately, he could swim and managed to climb out of the lake to safety. Friends rushed him home. After he had consumed what seemed like gallons of hot coffee, he stopped shivering, climbed into warm, dry clothes, and . . . returned for more skating!

When the deep snows came, coasting replaced skating as the sport of choice. Frank Stillman owned a large horse-drawn bobsled for hauling shingle bolts to the mill pond. Every year when heavy snows came, he hitched up his team and took folks for moonlight sleigh rides. The bobsled, which held about twenty people in its straw-covered bottom, announced its arrival with familiar sleigh bells. Laughter, songs, taffy, and popcorn added to the fun under an entourage of stars. With her knack for expressing things beautifully, Jenny whispered to Laura, "The stars twinkle like candles in a cathedral." Indeed, near Christmas the candlelit evergreen trees shining through windows added a special glow.

Besides skating and coasting, Jenny, Alvin, Laura, Little Star, the Brice boys, and many others enjoyed games of fox and geese, hare and hound, and ice hockey. Winter offered a time to slow down and the freedom for more leisure than in the growing and harvesting seasons. Often twenty or thirty gathered at a home for all types of indoor games, with charades being the favorite.

Although normally only about two feet of snow stayed on the ground, this winter turned out to be the worst in the history of Three Rivers. The town awakened in early March to *fifty-two inches of snow,* a depth that paralyzed many residents until Frank Stillman fashioned a V-shaped snowplow from heavy timbers. In a few hours he and his trusty helpers had cleared the roadways enough for school to be held, to the dismay of the youngsters who had hoped for an unscheduled holiday.

During the sleighrides the boys and young men scrambled to sit next to Jenny, Laura, and Little Star. Alvin Thomas usually won the place next to Jenny. One night she lifted her face to the sky and whispered, "I wish we could just ride forever. It is so beautiful."

"I do, too, Jenny." Something in Alvin's voice brought her out of her dreaming. Panic ran through her veins. *Would Alvin propose?* she wondered worriedly. She quickly called out, "Let's sing." In the jolly harmony she managed to convince herself nothing new had been in Alvin's words. Yet her heart knew better and a few days later she wasn't surprised when Alvin called and asked her to take a walk. At last the warm spring sun had succeeded in melting the snow.

"Jenny, I've always loved you. Could you ever learn to care?" he asked, his eyes steady.

"Oh, Alvin. You know I love you but not that way." Hot tears fell at the pain she saw in his face.

"It's all right," he told her sadly. "Somehow I didn't think you ever cared as I do. Is there someone else?"

She started to shake her head but then remembered how often her thoughts had turned to a young man who came out of the forest. "I don't know," she said miserably. "Can we still be friends?"

"Of course." He raised his head and smiled at her "Who knows? You may feel differently someday. If you don't, I love you enough to want you to be happy. If I can't be the one, then I hope you'll find a man who can."

For the rest of her life Jenny would associate soft, gray pussywillows and the familiar honking of wild geese flying northward with the cleanshaven young man who would put aside his own desires for her ultimate happiness.

In early May Jenny rode in to visit Little Star, pick up the mail, and go on to see Laura. At the General Store, which also served as a post office, she learned Sam

Grimsley had died a few days before. She immediately went to see Daddy O'Toone.

"Would you and Laura and Little Star sing a song or two at the funeral service?" the white-haired patriarch asked. "You've sung together before and do it so well to the glory of God."

Jenny agreed and contacted the others immediately. The day of the funeral turned out warm and sunny, yet a feeling of emptiness blanketed the inside of the white-steepled church and filled the half-dozen mourners. The only flowers consisted of a large bouquet of wild trilliums, purple violets, rosy bleeding-hearts, and johnny jumpups the young women had picked and placed on the forlorn gray casket. Sunbeams slipped through the stained-glass window as Daddy prayed and gave a short sermon that generated reverence and pity for the lonely Mr. Grimsley. At the conclusion of the service, Daddy, Doc Blanchard, Ben Shipley, and Andrew Ashley laid the unpopular old man to rest in the village cemetery where trees whispered secrets and wildflowers nodded.

The next day a notice of the upcoming Literary Society meeting appeared in the General Store, with an added note that everyone should attend if at all possible.

"It must be important," Jenny told Laura when they had gathered into the crowded schoolhouse. "And why is Doc up by the speaker's stand? What's he doing with that coffee can?"

"I don't know," Laura whispered back. Little Star on Laura's other side said, "He's acted strange all day."

Doc stood once the meeting had been called to order. "You all know Sam Grimsley died last week."

A raucous voice called from the back, "Guess nobody will miss him, hey, Doc?"

Doc Blanchard turned an icy stare in the direction of the uncouth young man who had no respect for the dead. "I would appreciate not being interrupted, sir." He coughed. "I discovered something in Mr. Grimsley's home you all should hear." He lifted the coffee can and removed a piece of paper.

To the people of Three Rivers:

Doc has told me I won't live long. I'm sorry for being unfriendly, especially to the children. If you know why, perhaps you'll forgive me. I once had a dear wife and two sons, six and eight. While out of town on a survey years

134

ago, I received notice to go home immediately. I did, and learned my family had died in a fire set by careless boys smoking in the dry grass behind what had been our home.

Since then I couldn't stand having children come near me. It brought back too many painful memories. Forgive me.

Sam Grimsley

Doc cleared his throat. "A clipping told the whole story. The family was apparently asleep and by the time firemen came, the whole house had become an inferno."

Jenny wanted to bury her face in her hands and cry. The looks on many faces around her showed others felt the same. That poor, poor man. If only they had known. . . .

Doc slowly turned the coffee can over. A tobacco sack fell out. He loosed the drawstring. Out tumbled nickels, dimes, pennies, and a few two-bit and four-bit pieces (twenty-five and fifty cents). "There's twenty-seven dollars total," Doc said huskily. In total silence he reached for the note again and read.

P.S. Please use the money to buy

*presents for the children of Three
Rivers. My boys would have liked that.*

Doc sat down heavily. Neighbor refused
to look at neighbor. Then Ben Shipley pro-
posed, "Let's honor Mr. Grimsley by
changing our May Day to Grimsley Day."

The people unanimously agreed but a
small boy piped up, "I guess he wasn't mean
after all, was he?" The meeting ended on a
serious note. Jenny suspected that never
again would her beloved town be so quick to
judge a stranger.

Spring transformed Three Rivers from
wintry silence to warm, jubilant activity.
The shingle and saw mills ran full blast.
Miners and prospectors busily loaded their
burros and pack mules for treks into the
hills. Hobble-skirted women purchased
yarn for knitting and gingham for new
spring dresses. Children played in the
schoolyard at recess. Afternoons found
folks congregated at the little red depot,
spinning yarns and waiting for the Galloping Goose.

Jenny rode to town one fine day to buy
suitable clothing for her lookout job and to
have White Knight fitted with shoes. She
left him at the blacksmith shop, ran lightly

along the rickety boardwalk and slipped and fell in a heap. Physically unhurt, her face flamed with injured pride.

"Are you hurt, lass?" a friendly voice inquired. Two strong arms lifted her gently to her feet.

"Why, it's big Jim Callihan!" Jenny smiled at the logger and straightened her skirts. "What are you doing here?"

"I came yesterday and now I'm on my way back to camp. Do you have time for lunch?"

"Of course." She gladly trotted alongside him as they made their way to Biddy Reed's. After they were served, she laughed at his whispered confession that ever since she pounded him on the back he'd been mighty careful about telling folks what he did for a living. A few minutes later she got back at him.

"How come you're not at the camp waiting tables?" He reached for his mug of hot coffee and took a healthy gulp.

"Soon I'm going to be busy sitting in a crows'-nest."

For a minute she thought he really was choking when the coffee evidently went "down the wrong pipe." During the remainder of their lunch she explained her new job then she excused herself. "I have to go to the ranger station and learn how to use a fire finder," she told him as she stood to leave.

"Good luck, lassie." He respectfully tipped his hat to her after paying the bill and followed her outside.

"And to you."

What an exciting day, Jenny thought a little later. The fire finder hadn't been complicated and she learned how to operate it in a short time. A simple device, it was essential to the lookouts in locating fires. Her thoughts turned to Keith Burgess. *He said he'd be working for the forest service again this summer,* she pondered. *I wonder what he will think when he doesn't find me at the logging camp? Will he visit Flower Dome, by any chance?* For the first time, her outlook dimmed a bit.

Since Flower Dome was far lower than Pinnacle Peak or Liberty Bell, the snow always melted at least two weeks earlier there. That meant the lookout firewatcher went to work sooner than at the other two crows'-nests. On a warm June day in the valley Jenny bid her parents goodbye and left Three Rivers astride White Knight. Despite the evident eagerness of Tammy trotting along beside them, the realization of what lay ahead sat heavy on her shoulders. What if she were homesick? How could she stand not seeing dear Laura all summer? Was this really God's will?

Halfway up the mountainside a crystal clear pond set in lush emerald grass offered a perfect spot to eat the sandwiches tucked away in her saddlebag and allow her horse and dog to rest. She hungrily bit into a sandwich and watched a doe and two tiny spotted fawns emerge from the trees across the pond. Still as a statue, she offered no threat and the deer came forward to drink, her fawns still a bit wobbly. "Maybe I'll write a book about the mountains and all the wild creatures that dwell here," Jenny mused aloud when the trio unhurriedly slipped back into the forest.

They reached Flower Dome by late afternoon, Jenny weary but in high spirits. Had any place ever been so lovely? She reveled in the thought she'd be spending the summer surrounded by such panoramic beauty. She unsaddled White Knight and tethered him and then telephoned the Three Rivers Station to let them know she'd arrived. Larry Benson had packed in her supplies and extra clothing a week before so everything lay ready and waiting for her.

Jenny found housekeeping in a crows'-nest different from at home. She cooked and heated with a kerosene stove. Water had to be fetched from an underground spring that bubbled out of the ground 500 yards downhill. As she kept a constant vigil for signs of fire, she found herself writing about her surroundings. From her vantage point, she had a clear view of the entire Stilliguamish Valley. Every day as she watched the Galloping Goose wind its way along the shore of the river she recalled the day she returned to Three Rivers. Was it a century ago, or just a year?

Jenny came to consider the different peaks — White Horse, Liberty Bell, the Suiattle range, Bedal, Sloan, Pinnacle Peak — her personal friends. Yet her pride and joy towered high above the others: the majestic Glacier Peak.

The first two weeks passed uneventfully and then one afternoon she noticed strange light flashes coming from Pinnacle Peak. They appeared with some regularity for twenty or thirty minutes. Puzzled and curious, she phoned in to the ranger station. No direct line ran between the lookouts. All calls went through the village exchange and interference on the line at times made it difficult to hear. It took several minutes to contact the station.

"Hello. Ranger station."

"This is Jenny on Flower Dome."

"Matt Davis. What's on your mind?"

"I just wanted to report strange flashes of light on top of Pinnacle Peak."

"Talk louder, Jenny. I can't hear you. Are you reporting a fire?"

"No, I see light flashes on Pinnacle Peak," she shouted.

"Thanks. I'll call and see if the lookout there can see anything. I'll call you back."

Jenny breathlessly waited until the phone rang. This time Matt Davis came in loud and clear and chuckling. "The lookout man says he's signaling you with his mirror, saying hello."

"He *what?*" Jenny could scarcely believe her ears.

"Keith is signaling you," Matt patiently repeated.

"Keith who?" Jenny's heart thumped.

"Keith Burgess, the lookout. Said he knew you."

"Uh, he does." Dazed, Jenny said goodbye. Moments later she grabbed the wall mirror and ran outside her crows'-nest. As she caught the sun's rays and flashed a message toward Pinnacle Peak, little did she know she had begun a steady correspondence. After that, the mirrors busily sent messages between the two crows'-nests each day. Neither crows'-nest resident could spell out words but Jenny felt sure the young man who loomed large in her thoughts was sending love letters. The thought brought a rich blush to her cheeks when she admitted to White Knight and Tammy, "If Alvin asked me now if I cared for someone else, I'd have to answer yes."

Jenny loved her job, yet as the Fourth of July neared she missed Three Rivers. Who would win the horse race this year? Not White Knight, growing fat and lazy from grazing. A little pang went through her. If only she had met Keith that fateful day. Suddenly she felt violently homesick, as miserable as when she left for school all those years ago.

"Stop moping and get busy," she told herself out loud. "Work is the best remedy for the doldrums." She rode White Knight down the trail to get fresh water. Tammy gamboled through the wildflowers then stopped and barked just before they reached the spring. Jenny saw nothing to cause such a commotion. She turned. That couldn't be voices. Her heart leaped. Horses rounded the bend in the trail and on their backs were Laura and Little Star.

"Oh, I am so glad you came!" Water forgotten, Jenny ran to her friends, all three talking at once.

Once at the lookout, Laura could contain herself no longer. "Do we have news for you!"

"What?"

"Remember that nice young man we met at camp last summer? He stopped by again a few weeks ago to see you. He turned pale as a ghost when I told him you weren't there, but lit up like a harvest moon after he learned you had the Flower Dome lookout this summer."

"I talk with him every day," Jenny boasted, to hide the little bounce of her heart.

"Sure you do, Jenny, and I'm Pocahontas," Little Star put in. "Laura, think the loneliness here has affected her brain?"

"I really do," Jenny insisted. She demonstrated with the mirror and the friends laughed delightedly when answering flashes came.

"What do you say to each other?" Little Star giggled and nudged Laura.

Jenny smiled, too happy to resent teasing. "I'll never tell. How long can you stay?"

"Until noon tomorrow."

The hours fled like shadows before a rising sun. The crows'-nest had no guest accommodations, so the friends slept in the soft grass outside, talking until far into the night and waking early to chatter on. Jenny felt more alone than ever when they left. To revive her spirits, she spent some time writing, cherishing all the while what Laura had said about Keith.

As July blazed out and August sweltered in, Jenny was put to the supreme test of a good firewatcher. While scanning the horizon she observed an ominous black cloud approaching from the west. The twin sister of the storm Keith had lived through the year before now attacked the area. Jagged lightning fingers tore trees asunder and thunder cracked like giant crashing boulders. Jenny knew the crows'-nest was well grounded with copper wires and rods to prevent danger, so she got into bed and waited.

Lightning struck the copper rod atop her dwelling. Blue tongues of fire leaped between pots and pans. The crows'-nest quivered like a saucer of gelatin. This time no rain followed. As the lightning wreaked havoc, Jenny kept busy calculating the locations of several spot fires with her fire finder. When she finished sending in reports to headquarters on one fire, she would begin taking sightings of the next. She knew Matt Davis and his crews would be hard-put to extinguish the fires, especially those in remote areas.

When Larry Benson brought in fresh supplies he had news of a raging fire near the crest of the Cascade Divide between the Snoqualmie and Lake Wenatchee forest districts. "The terrain's so rugged from the base camp where there's water, it takes all day to reach the fire that's only a mile away," he reported. He went on to explain that the saplings were so intertwined that the forest was more like a jungle. At times the firefighters had to crawl several feet off the ground over dense brush, all the while shouldering heavy, tool-laden backpacks. The only water was a quarter of a mile downhill from the fire. Jenny was amazed to hear him say that the firefighters slept with their feet propped against a tree to keep from sliding downhill. Days later Jenny learned from headquarters the fire had been conquered, but not without bad burns and broken bones. She rejoiced when her prayers for rain ended with a downpour.

Her stay on Flower Dome was nearly over and she knew she would miss her cozy crows'-nest. "On the other hand," she announced to her faithful animal friends when they went down the mountainside, "we'll get to see the lookout from Pinnacle Peak soon." Flashing signals between mountain peaks had been fun and exciting. Meeting Keith Burgess again in person was a different story. Would it be as thrilling as her heart predicted? Should she be casual or warm and outgoing? She settled her heart as she always had done: "Help me to be natural, God, and to know Your will."

Nine

Keith Burgess approached the fork in the road. He knew that Jennifer Ashley must ride down this very road on her way to report to the ranger station in Three Rivers. A few casual questions to Matt Davis, which he realized hadn't fooled his supervisor in the least, had elicited this information about Jenny's return.

The days since he left Pinnacle Peak had been busy ones. If the young woman he loved cared for him, he had a surprise for her, arranged since he came down from the lookout. "I'll just be casual," he muttered. "There's a big difference between flashing mirrors and expecting Jenny to love me." A glint came into his blue eyes and his smile stretched wide. He reached into his pocket and brought out a round object. It shouldn't be long now.

"Remember," he warned himself out loud, "don't rush things. She's only seen you once."

Jenny and White Knight, with Tammy close behind, rode into sight. Keith raised the small round mirror and captured the sun's rays. They flashed onto Jenny's surprised face and highlighted the glow in her brown eyes, and the telltale red that crept up from the collar of her jacket.

"Why, Keith," she faltered. She reined White Knight in, slipped from the saddle, and held out both hands.

His good intentions cast aside, in a moment Keith had both arms around her. "Oh, Jenny, I love you so," he whispered.

She didn't speak.

Dread filled his heart. What a fool he had been, a presumptuous, bold fool! He released her and stepped back, feeling a wave of color sweep into his face. "Forgive me, Miss Ashley, Jenny." Was that babbling voice *his?* "I'm sorry."

"You are?" She looked shocked.

"It's just that ever since I first saw you I've felt you are the woman God intended for me," Keith said in a low voice. He glanced down but when she remained still for a long time, he squared his shoulders and looked into her eyes again.

"Then why are you sorry?" A small smile curled Jenny's lips and settled in Keith's heart.

"You mean . . . ?" He had trouble getting the words out.

"If I hadn't c-cared, do you think I would have been so immodest as to flash signals to you all summer?" A diamond drop sparkled in the long lashes that now rested delicately on her pink cheeks.

He opened his arms and she ran into them, returning his tight embrace. "Jenny," he said hoarsely, "will you marry me? I mean, someday when the time is right? Will you be my wife?"

"I will." Sometime in the future the actual wedding ceremony would come but her simple acceptance by the side of a dusty road pledged their love. Keith bent his head until their lips met, then held her close. *What a priceless treasure God has sent into my life! May I ever be worthy of her,* he silently prayed, then kissed her again.

"I have to report in and tell Matt I want the Flower Dome lookout next spring," she finally said, her face rosy and eyes shining. "Then you must come home with me for supper."

A little qualm went through Keith. "What will they say when we tell them we plan to be married?"

She hesitated, her clear eyes troubled. "Keith, I hope you'll see this my way, but

149

could we wait to announce our engagement? I'm not sure they'll understand how we can both be so certain this is right when they learn that until today, we had only spoken to each other one time."

Keith laughed easily and took her hands in his. "I understand completely."

She swung into the saddle and he walked along beside her. After making her final report at the ranger station, Jenny rejoined Keith near the tree where she had tethered White Knight.

"What time shall I ride out?" Keith asked, almost loath to let her out of his sight. He realized Jenny needed time to clean up and rest after her long trek from Flower Dome.

"Come any time after four. We have supper at five," she told him. A poignant light in her eyes set his heart thumping. Mindful of possible watching eyes, Keith contented himself with bowing over her hand before she rode away.

Jenny appreciated the speed with which her white stallion could cover the distance between the Ashley ranch and Three Rivers but today she held him in. Not only had they already traveled far, she needed time to savor the meeting at the fork of the road. How handsome Keith had looked, standing there smiling and waiting for her! He must have taken some pains to know her arrival time or he couldn't have been in exactly the right place at the right time. She thrilled again to the reverence in his eyes, and the boyish pleading when he asked her to marry him.

"Dear God, may I ever be a true wife," she whispered. "And may our lives together shine so You may be glorified." She rode the rest of the way home in a happy daze. Surely Mother and Father would like Keith! She crossed Browns Creek, teeming with humpback salmon. Once every four years the species migrated from the ocean to the upper reaches of rivers and streams to spawn their eggs in the same place where they were hatched. Although Jenny had taken the salmon for granted as she rode by, when Keith arrived promptly at four his reaction was quite the opposite. Jenny had met him in the meadow just across the rail fence, a vision in pink that had stirred his heart even more than hours earlier. After introductions were made, the smitten couple and Jenny's father walked to the creek.

"There must be millions churning the shallow riffles," Keith exclaimed. "I'll wager I could walk across on their backs without getting my feet wet!" He wrinkled his forehead. "I don't understand one thing, though. Once I tried to put some that had been forced out of the water to the sandy beach but they immediately thrust forward onto the bank."

"They beach themselves after spawning," Andrew Ashley explained. "They are created to end their life span so and make way for the new generation."

Later while Jenny and her mother finished getting dinner, Keith and Andrew sat and chatted inside the quaint log cabin. The beautiful handcrafted furniture had at first seemed primitive to Keith until he realized how well all the pieces complemented the rough-hewn setting. Picture frames had been carved from maple burls and highly polished. Handwoven rugs covered the floor. No fine walnut or mahogany furniture could possibly blend in with the great stone fireplace and warm, homey atmosphere. To think that the Ashleys had fashioned the rugs and furniture with their own hands! The visitor soberly reflected on how unimportant and meaningless many modern things were when compared to this log cabin filled with the love of God and one another.

His heart swelled. Someday he and Jenny would have a home where Jesus Christ reigned as head of the household. The thought warmed him even more than the heat from the well-planned fireplace with its flaming six-foot log sending smoke drifts up the enormous chimney.

After supper Jenny invited Keith for a ride. He admired the capable way she saddled White Knight while he resaddled the horse he had ridden from town. "Well, did I pass?"

Mischief sparkled in every movement of her slender body. "Yes, I could tell by the look they shared when we left for our ride. Now, Mr. Burgess, you may have graduated from the school of forestry but I can teach you some things about the woods that aren't in books or lessons."

"Such as what?" he challenged as he rode beside her.

"Do you know how to tell from a distance a hemlock from a fir?"

"N-oo. They look alike from far away," Keith admitted.

"Look at the tops," Jenny smugly said. "Hemlock tips hang down in an upside-down **U**. Firs point straight up."

Enchanted with the play of expressions on her face, he encouraged, "What else can you show me?"

Jenny pointed to a large maple. "If you remove the moss beneath the green fern growing out of it on the side of the tree you'll find licorice root. You can chew it or season food with it."

"You're amazing," he told her and she blushed.

"I'm sure you already know what those are." She waved toward several five-foot-tall thorny stalks with huge green leaves at the top. "Devil's club." She shuddered. "Never touch one. Little Star had to assist Doc Blanchard in the amputation of a finger when a man didn't get help right away."

"They are like sin," Keith put in. "Harmless looking but deadly." He changed the subject. "Jenny, I'm going to stay in Three Rivers for the winter. I have a job in the mill."

"That's wonderful!" She clapped her hands.

"How soon can we tell your folks . . . about us?"

Mischief danced in her eyes again. "I think they'll know when you escort me to church, come for Sunday dinner, that kind of thing."

"I want to act in the proper way and ask your father for your hand," Keith sturdily maintained.

"Then give them time to know you," she said practically. But there was nothing practical in the way she kissed him goodnight when it was time for Keith to return to town. Alone again with his horse, Keith thanked God for the love of this wonderful woman.

Several weeks later Jenny consented to Keith speaking with her father but insisted on being present, along with her mother. "It will make it easier," she told him.

Keith felt unaccountably nervous, although the Ashleys had long since made him feel very much at home. However, hospitality wasn't the same as giving a daughter in marriage. Despite all his preparation, when the time came Keith blurted out, "I want to tell you something. Sir, I love her. Will you marry me?"

Andrew grinned broadly and crossed his arms over his powerful chest. "Want to try that again?"

Keith took a deep breath. "I mean, will Jenny marry me? Oh, hang it, I love your daughter and she loves me. May we have your blessing?"

Jenny's father looked from the agitated Keith to Jenny, who tried to hide her mirth. Last of all he turned to his wife of so many years. "If you can make my daughter happy, as her mother has done me, then God bless you both, son." He pumped Keith's hand

and hugged Jenny. "Now, I want to give you some advice. Things worth having in life are worth fighting for. Don't be bashful. Just march right up and — why, when I was your age, I never let anything unnerve me."

Esther Ashley cocked her head to one side and said in an innocent voice, "Funny, I seem to remember the first time you took me for a buggy ride. You were so fussed you put the horse's collar on upside-down." Her husband couldn't help joining in the laughter at his expense.

One day when the mill shut down for repairs, Keith visited the woods to observe logging firsthand. A forest ranger should have a working knowledge of the harvesting of timber. He watched fallers down a Douglas fir a good six feet in diameter at the stump, thrilling as they shouted, "Timber!" He marveled at the stalwart buckers with their seven-foot saws and other paraphernalia needed to cut up the felled trees. The loggers worked like mules, paid according to their output: An average bucker cut between 18,000 and 25,000 board feet a day. One logger admitted that during a six-month period, he bucked an average of 40,000 feet of lumber a day.

The danger of yarding the logs from the woods to the landing was evident. Keith stood near a worker called a "whistle punk" who had to be out of danger yet where he could observe operations at all times. The unsung hero of logging camps, the whistle punk sent signals by jerking a wire attached to the donkey whistle. Men's lives depended on the accuracy of the signals the whistle punk sent.

Just before Thanksgiving Keith experienced another exciting part of Three Rivers life. Jenny asked him, "How would you like to win a bird?"

"Well, I sat in a crows'-nest so I'm *game* for most anything," he retorted and laughed at his pun.

"Now's your chance." She pointed to a large poster in the General Store that announced the annual turkey shoot.

"What's a turkey shoot? Are there wild turkeys in the woods?"

Jenny shook her head and looked solemn but her lips twitched. "There's still a little flatland furriner in you, I see. No, this is a marksmanship contest. You'll see excellent shooting and the winner gets a turkey, goose, or duck. Each man pays fifty cents to enter."

"How can folks shoot accurately with the firearms I've seen?" Keith demanded suspiciously. "Many of them aren't that far removed from the old squirrel rifles their grandfathers used."

She smiled and raised one eyebrow. "Just wait and see."

The morning of the contest snow began to fall. In Keith's mind, the large and feathery flakes would make shooting difficult; luck, rather than fine marksmanship, might determine the winner.

Uncle Ben Shipley, who had welcomed Keith into his home many times, appeared with his trusty 30-30. One of the better shots, he made an unusual move. "Why don't you try, son?" He held out his gun.

Keith flushed with pleasure. Old-timers seldom loaned their guns and this was a high compliment. "Thanks, but you would do better."

"Go ahead, for Jenny." He motioned to the bright-eyed young woman on the sidelines. "Now, when you get the front bead lined up with the bottom of the **V** in the rear sight and both are lined up with the bottom of the bull's-eye, press the trigger gently."

Keith followed the older man's instructions exactly, squinting through the snow. Disappointment surged through him when he fired; he was sure he'd missed the target completely. He bit his lip and wished he had refused Uncle Ben's generous offer. The next moment the crowd cheered when the judge called out, "Number seven wins."

"That's you, son." A wide grin split Ben Shipley's face.

Keith didn't believe it until the judge shoved a fourteen-pound turkey into his arms. The contest continued, but for the first year in several, Uncle Ben didn't win a bird. Keith insisted on giving his prize to the Shipleys. They promptly invited him and the Ashleys for Thanksgiving dinner.

Thanksgiving dawned clear and cold. Jenny donned a warm, bright-flowered dress with lace collar and a charming hat. Keith wore a new gray suit, high celluloid collar, derby hat, and polished button shoes. Heads turned when they drove down Main Street with the older Ashleys.

Laura teased the young man about his mirrored signals but Keith just grinned. "We'll be sending real signals next year," he promised, as he proffered a book from his pocket.

Jenny read the title aloud and burst into laughter. Keith's book was on the Morse code!

"I got the idea at the depot yesterday, watching the agent send telegraph messages," he explained. "Mirrors won't be as accurate as a telegraph key but they'll serve our purpose."

They gathered around the well-laden table with its golden-skinned turkey in the center flanked by bowls of steaming food. "Let us join hands and give thanks," Ben Shipley said. A knock stopped them. Laura excused herself and went to the door. The family waited for her return. Instead they heard a scream of joy and moments later Laura and Donald Ashley appeared, both wearing smiles. The turkey Uncle Ben didn't win in the shoot had to wait while everyone exclaimed over their surprise visitor. His ship in dry dock, Don would be home for several weeks.

The Ashleys capped off the day by officially announcing the engagement of Jenny and Keith. Don reached under the table, slid something cool onto Laura's ring finger, and then stood. "They aren't the only ones!"

More good news poured in. The mill had reluctantly laid off some of the latest hired but Jake Lieberman offered Keith a job clerking in his store.

"I have to be honest," Keith told him. "Next June I'll be back working for the forest service."

Jake didn't care. He needed someone to

help with inventory and by the following summer he could find a new clerk.

Jenny couldn't ever remember being happier. She and Keith and Don and Laura became inseparable. They talked of a possible double wedding sometime in the future. When winter came, heightened by the tang of love, skating and coasting and sleigh riding became even more joyous. Her heart constricted once when Keith took a terrible fall off a sled on its way downhill. If anything ever happened to him . . . she refused to complete the thought. Her heart burst with pride when they joined hands in prayer over meals or talked about God and His plan for them.

Jake Lieberman told the Ladies Aid Society just before Christmas that if they would make bags, he'd furnish netting and enough candy and nuts to fill them so every child could have a treat at the annual Christmas program held in the church. The women also made a large banner that proclaimed PEACE ON EARTH, GOOD WILL TO MEN and strung it across the front of the church. A New Year's Eve dance was carefully monitored so no one who had imbibed in spirits could come in.

Keith noticed how Three Rivers folk cared for their own, even in little things.

Once at a box social, Jake Lieberman purchased a beautiful box that contained only a large chunk of bologna and several slices of sparsely buttered rye bread.

"My favorite!" he exclaimed to the shabbily dressed young woman who had brought the only thing she could afford.

Keith also knew how much credit the good storekeeper gave. When he mentioned it, Jake shrugged. "The people will pay when they get back to work." The discussion had ended but Keith felt even fonder than before of his employer.

All too quickly Don's leave ended and he prepared to report back to his ship. Still, the fact the young merchant marine would soon attain his captain's stripes mellowed Laura's sorrow. Once done, they would marry and never have to be apart again.

Keith and Jenny did not accompany Don and Laura to the depot the morning Don left town. Long after the Galloping Goose departed, Laura stood watching the tracks, shivering in the cold morning air. The depot agent came outside to check some waybills. "Are you all right, miss?"

Laura didn't answer.

"Can I help you, young lady?" The man touched her shoulder.

Laura looked at the concerned agent like

one arriving home from a faraway country. "No, but thank you." She turned and walked away, knowing the kindly man's gaze followed her but unable to say more.

Ten

"Keith!" Jenny ran to meet him one spring evening when he rode to the ranch, her voice bubbling over with enthusiasm. "One of the outfits is going to top a spar tree Sunday afternoon not far from here. Would you like to go? I've never seen it done and it's supposed to be exciting." Tendrils of hair that had escaped her luxuriant braid curled around her eager face.

"I'd love to go anywhere, anytime, as long as it's with you."

His fervent answer brought laughter and a warm pink to her cheeks and on Sunday, along with half the town, they hiked out to witness this rare event. The tree selected had been stripped of branches the day before. Now a small, wiry man wearing steel leg braces with four-inch spurs and a twenty-five-foot rope with a steel core began throwing the loop of the rope upward so he could literally walk up the naked tree trunk by kicking his spurs into the wood.

164

The higher he climbed, the more nervous Jenny felt. What if he slipped and the belt didn't catch him? The point where he stopped to make his cut was more than a hundred feet high. She sighed with relief when he double-checked his safety belt and thrust his spurs deep into the tree, then began chopping an undercut. (An undercut, a notch on the opposite side of the tree from where the main cut will be made, is used to ensure that the tree will fall in the proper direction.)

"The steel core in the rope prevents him from accidentally chopping it in two," a nearby logger explained.

As wood chips fell, the tension mounted. Local photographers attempted to capture the daring young man. Soon the familiar cry came, "Timber-r-r-r!" Jenny's eyes never wavered from the man. The top of the tree swayed, broke away, and fell, leaving the tree swinging violently.

"Oh, no!" Jenny clutched Keith's arm. "Look!"

The intrepid high climber stood on the still-swaying tree, waving to the crowd. A few moments later, instead of coming down one foot at a time, he loosened the rope loop, kicked free his spurs, and dropped fifteen or twenty feet at once, finally reaching the ground. Jenny whispered to Keith, "Promise me you'll never try anything like that."

"My dear girl, I have no desire to top a tree," he told her.

Due to an unusually hot spring and summer, the lookout firewatchers were ordered to their crow's-nests early. Temperatures in the valley rose to over 90 degrees daily and even at the crows'-nests with their high elevation the heat became unbearable. With a humidity of only 21 percent an explosive situation developed. Jenny got to hate the morning weather report from headquarters, "Continued hot and dry." Usually hot spells in Three Rivers lasted not more than a week but now two weeks had gone by, with each day worse than the one before. Jenny's job had grown monotonous. With the increased fire danger, she had no time for anything that would detract her from constant surveillance of the district.

A third week passed. Jenny groaned and scanned her area again. Something caught her eye. She hesitated. Was it smoke? Lookouts had to make positive identification and send in accurate reports. A few times a lookout had reported a fire that turned out to be a small fog bank. Jenny reached for her binoculars. It *was* smoke. She quickly took a reading on her fire finder and relayed it to Three Rivers, knowing they would immediately call Keith on Pinnacle Peak so he could take a bearing.

High and safe in her crows'-nest, Jenny's heart went out to those who fought the fire. The ranger station reported they had recruited every available man in Three Rivers to fight the devouring force, now out of control. Intense heat had generated a chimney-like effect that caused the fire to flare even more violently. "A hundred acres charred the first day," she whispered to Tammy that evening. "If they can keep it inside the logged-off fire trail they made, it will stop. If it gets into the timber. . . ." She shuddered.

After a brief respite overnight, an ember carried to a nearby cedar tree killed all hopes of an early victory. The cedar exploded into a flaming torch that triggered off a dreaded crown fire. Racing across the top of the forest like a tidal wave, the crown fire became a roaring wall of flame that sent deer and other animals fleeing for their lives. On Flower Dome Jenny watched in horror as the great clouds of dense black smoke plumed into the air. She could tell by the color of the smoke the fire had reached virgin green timber.

On the third day a thousand acres were

burning out of control.

On the fourth day news arrived that a small group of firefighters was trapped inside the fire. Jenny prayed with all her heart. Her father, Alvin, Ben Shipley, and dozens of other friends were out there fighting. Were they among the trapped men? Sobbing, she thanked God that Keith remained on Pinnacle Peak. "Please forgive me for my selfishness."

"We're setting back fires," came the ranger station report.

Jenny prayed again. Through her binoculars she could see ant-sized men digging wide trenches, then hundreds of small fires flaring when set along their edge on the side nearest the fire. The desperate measure worked. By the time the main fire reached the trenches, the small fires had gobbled up all flammable material. With no new fuel, the fire came under control, although it took days to stamp out the remaining embers. Jenny thanked God again when it turned out to be only a rumor and no crew had been trapped. But she shook her head when a weary-sounding Matt Davis reported that untold millions of board feet of fine timber had been lost, and all because of a careless smoker who dropped his cigarette.

Jenny had never been in danger on Flower

Dome but for a time she could see neither Three Rivers nor Pinnacle Peak due to heavy acrid smoke that blotted out the sun in those directions. A few days later a drenching rain healed the parched land and life became normal once more.

The summer ended. Jenny and Keith returned home and he went back to work in the lumber mill, gaining more experience in the logging game. Christmas came and went, then January. In mid-February when Jenny and her parents drove to town in the buggy to attend church, she was surprised that none of the Shipleys had come. She whispered to Little Star, who sat next to her in the choir, "Where's Laura?"

"I don't know." The young Indian woman looked worried. "There's a lot of sickness around. Let's go see if the Shipleys are all right after church." Hours later as they entered the Shipley home, the pungent smell of turpentine greeted them. Laura lay propped up in her bed, her chest covered with a flannel cloth over lard and turpentine to rid the body of congestion.

"I thought you'd come," she croaked, eyes bright and red fever spots on her cheeks. "Don't get near me. I'm contagious."

"I'll be back tomorrow," Jenny promised and Little Star added, "I'll tell Doc

Blanchard to come too."

"I don't need him," Laura said but after Jenny went into the other room Aunt Carrie told the young nurse to send Doc when he could spare the time.

The next morning after breakfast Jenny saddled White Knight and rode to the Shipleys. Doc Blanchard's buggy stood near the front gate. Jenny knew Doc tended to fuss over his patients and keep a close check on them. She stabled White Knight and ran to the house through lightly sifting snow. "How's Laura?" she asked when she got inside.

"Running a fever." Doc took liquid and pills from his worn black bag. "Give her two pills every four hours for fever and a tea-spoonful of liquid as needed for the cough. Keep her warm and break the fever. I'll be back tonight." He grunted. "Seems like half the town's down with sniffles. Now the grippe's starting."

Jenny slipped in for just a few minutes with Laura, who squeezed her hand tight. Her blue eyes shone with the sisterly love they had shared. Jenny slipped out and spent the rest of the day helping Aunt Carrie. By night when Doc returned, the fever had lowered a bit but Jenny saw his quickly hidden look of dismay and caught a husky note in his voice when he told them they'd know more in the morning. He arrived about ten and went straight to Laura. He stayed for what seemed an eternity to Jenny and when he came out he sat down heavily in a chair.

"I don't want to frighten you but Laura is a very sick girl. It's grippe, and her lungs are quite congested. Keep giving her the medicine, and pray. I'll send Little Star out."

Jenny tried to warm herself but she felt chilled to the bone. When at last Little Star arrived, she whispered, "I feel so helpless. All I can do is pray."

"My father and mother are speaking of her to the Great Spirit as well," Little Star said. A great warm drop splashed to Jenny's hand when the other woman put her arm around her. Jenny choked back a sob. Never before had she seen Little Star cry. She clung to her friend and thanked God for her presence during that day and night.

Early the next morning it began to snow and by midafternoon six inches covered the ground. Ben Shipley kept huge logs in the fireplace to warm against the wintry blast. Doc and Aunt Carrie kept vigil at Laura's bedside. Jenny and Little Star sat close together, not speaking, while Jenny's mind traveled back through all the years with Laura.

A ray of sunlight brought her back to the present and she ran to the window. "Why, it's stopped snowing!" The sunbeam shone straight at the house for just a minute and then the clouds closed and snow began falling again. The bedroom door creaked behind Jenny. She turned, knowing what she would hear.

"I'm sorry." Doc Blanchard looked old and beaten.

Too wounded for tears, Jenny thought of how the sun had shone through the storm for a single moment. Laura's ladder to heaven had been revealed to them.

She bid Uncle Ben and Aunt Carrie goodbye and put on her woolen coat, cap, and mittens. Little Star followed her to the barn and helped her saddle White Knight. After Jenny mounted, she placed one hand on Jenny's mittened one. A lovely light shone in her still-damp dark eyes. "I never can and won't try to take her place," she said simply. "But Jenny, we know we'll see her again. That's the hope Jesus offers. Until then, you still have me."

Her words released a spring inside Jenny. Scalding tears fell to White Knight's mane. Little Star just patted Jenny's hand.

"Th-thank you," Jenny finally managed to say. She clasped her hand then rode into the swirling snow. A sad task remained and it would take all the encouragement and help of God to perform it. That night she wrote the most difficult letter of her life.

> *Dear Don,*
> *My heart aches as I write this sad news. A few days ago dear Laura fell ill. Doc Blanchard said it was grippe. Late this afternoon God took her to be with Him.*
> *I know this will come as a terrible shock to you. How little I can say, yet I want to tell you something. Before Laura died snow had been falling so steadily I could barely see the barn. Suddenly the blizzard stopped and a beam of sunlight shone on the house for just a minute. Then the snow began again.*
> *When Doc came out of Laura's room I already knew what he would say. The sunbeam was the hand of God reaching down to take Laura.*
> *I don't know when this letter will catch you. I do remember your saying you'd be sailing through the Panama Canal so I will send it there.*
> *With love and sympathy from all of us,*
>
> *Jenny*

Keith and Little Star spent as much time with Jenny as possible in the next few weeks. She faithfully attended church every Sunday but no longer sang in the choir. At least for now she found sitting in the choir loft too hard without Laura. She welcomed each passing day that brought her nearer to her third year on Flower Dome. There she found solace in work. With a cooler summer there were only a few small brush fires to report and Jenny found time for writing.

One day she received a wonderful surprise. Tammy barked furiously and heralded the approach of Little Star and Big Bear.

"It is good to remember," Big Bear said at their campfire in the meadow that evening as he talked of happy times with Laura.

Her heart filled to bursting, Jenny agreed. Reliving the wonderful trip to Glacier Peak, the funny things that happened, and Laura's joyful spirit helped break the shackles of sadness that had bound her. She nodded in understanding when Little Star said softly, "If we do not speak of Laura, it is as if she never lived. When we remember, she still lives in our hearts."

Their visit had light moments as well. Big Bear chuckled when he saw how Keith and Jenny talked with each other using their mirrors. He admitted he'd never seen anything like it.

Summer slipped away so rapidly Jenny could scarcely believe when she was told to pack up and vacate her crows'-nest for another year. She rejoiced that Keith had a letter waiting from the regional office of the U.S. Forest Service. Increased logging and timber sales in the region required new personnel. His qualifications plus an excellent report from Matt Davis had won Keith the job of district ranger. Jenny glowed with pride.

Months sped by. When spring came again Jenny realized Laura had been gone for more than a year. One Sunday Jenny announced she wasn't going to church, an unprecedented decision.

"Are you ill?" Her mother peered at her.

"No. I want to visit Pixie House."

Esther Ashley patted her daughter's shoulder and hurried out to the buggy. Jenny hadn't gone to her childhood playhouse since before Laura died.

She wandered sadly to the little house and sat down inside, Tammy at her feet. She could almost hear Laura calling, "Jenny, Jenny, I'm here," as she had done so many times before. She remembered what Little Star had said months ago at Flower Dome and months before that at the Shipleys.

We know we'll see her again. That's the hope Jesus offers. . . . When we remember, she still lives in our hearts.

"Dear God," Jenny prayed. "I thank You I came here today. I thank You that because You sent Your Only Son to die for us, it will only be a little while before I can be with dear Laura again forever and with You. Little Star is right. Laura will always live in my heart and memories. Help me to live for You, as she did. In Jesus' name. Amen."

Jenny left Pixie House feeling happier and more at peace than she had in a long time. Strength to leave the past behind, although she would never forget it, and to face the future with her head up and chin high sent her flying to meet her parents' buggy. She knew they had worried about her and she couldn't help noticing the great relief in their faces when she told them she was all right.

Now she sang about her work. She prayed for help and went to choir practice. She sang with the choir, flanked by Little Star on one side and memories of Laura on the other. The two sang duets when asked and always the assurance of eternal life with her Master, family, and friends sustained Jenny.

Because of Keith's upcoming promotion

Jenny decided she would only spend one more summer in the Flower Dome crows'-nest. Following that, she and Keith would marry and establish a home of their own in their beloved Three Rivers, perhaps even on some of the Ashley land. With the normal anticipation of a young woman deeply in love, who knows that love is of God and acceptable to Him, she began to make her plans. The next weeks floated by in a drift of happiness. But as Keith and Jenny dreamed their dreams, neither realized how soon those crystalline hopes would be shattered.

Eleven

April 6, 1917, began like any other spring day in Three Rivers. Hardy loggers climbed aboard the crummy for the long ride to the woods. Saws in the lumber mill whirred. Horses and wagons kicked up dust clouds up and down Main Street. Folks casually shopped and the tantalizing aroma of fresh bakery goods from Biddy Reed's mingled with the morning air. Jenny finished her chores early and rode White Knight into town, glad to be out in the rain-washed world.

By midafternoon all traces of tranquil normalcy had disappeared. Over the telegraph the tragic news reached Three Rivers: *The United States declares war on Germany.* Carried at first by a dozen voices, and then a hundred, the fateful words sped to the woods and logging camps. Jake Lieberman stood in his General Store, tears pouring freely down his weathered cheeks. What would this mean to him, a man of German ancestry whose life and heart belonged to America?

Keith Burgess sat stunned at the ranger station. Every plan he and Jenny had lovingly made turned to ashes.

Alvin Thomas and dozens like him set their jaws. If their country needed them, they would gladly lay down tools and lives to defend the freedom, liberty, and justice on which America had been formed.

Jenny and her parents bravely went about their daily duties, although visibly shaken. What did the future hold for Donald? Where was he now? The letter about Laura's death had long since been answered in a brokenhearted scrawl, but now weeks had passed since they had heard from him.

Little Star and Big Bear also faced pain. Some of the tribe would undoubtedly serve in the military. Not a family in Three Rivers could escape the results of a man mad with power who longed to control the world.

Long before the government began recruiting men between twenty-one and thirty, dozens of local men, including Keith, had scorned the draft and enlisted. After initial examinations they were sent home to await orders. A week later Keith received notice he must report to Camp Lewis for basic training. What a far cry from the happy summer he and Jenny had planned! The question in his heart was reflected in the anxious eyes of his comrades, their families, and friends: Would he, would any of them, come back? A pall settled on the community. No longer did the departure of the Galloping Goose attract gossiping crowds. Only those who came to bid farewell to sons and brothers — and to weep — came to the depot.

At last Jenny and Keith's turn came. Arm in arm they sat quietly huddled in one corner of the depot. They didn't talk; nothing remained to be said. Each tick of the clock seemed to stab her like a sharp knife. Hysteria threatened but she refused to give in. Keith must not leave with the memory of tears.

"I love you," she whispered.

"I love you, Jenny." He held her close and touched her beautiful hair. "Every day at noon, no matter where you are, flash your mirror and send me a message. I'll do the same."

"I will, I will," she promised.

"All aboard," the conductor bellowed. Keith kissed Jenny and climbed to the rear platform of the coach. Two blasts of the whistle and the Galloping Goose moved away. Jenny waved her lacy pink handkerchief until the train rounded a curve and disappeared.

The rigors of basic training left Keith no time to feel homesick. Lying on his bunk at night, his thoughts of home were blotted out with echoes of "squads right, column left, about-face, ten-shun!" Through the grapevine he learned that troops were so badly needed the men barely had time to learn maneuvers before being shipped out.

Humor played its part and lightened the grim atmosphere. A corporal who was a practical joker called Keith to one side his first day in boot camp and asked him if he had a can of shoe polish. "It's important to keep neat, you know. Listen, the supply sergeant has a few cans of special polish left. It lasts twice as long as regular issue. Tell him you want a can of cosmetic shoe polish."

Keith became the laughingstock of his company. He took the joke like the man he was and soon the men forgot it.

After two weeks' training in Company E of the Ninety-first Division, Keith was promised a three-day pass for the weekend. His elation was short-lived; the next day the order was rescinded and the entire division was assigned to quarters. Two days later the dreaded news came: They were being shipped overseas the next day.

Keith tried desperately to call Jenny and failed. Jammed telephone lines left him frustrated, but he did manage to write a letter. Shortly after midnight trucks transported the soldiers to the docks at Tacoma and Seattle where ships lay anchored and ready. No matter how far apart they would be, every day at noon Keith faithfully removed a small mirror from his pocket and flashed a message to his love.

"Whatcha doin', buddy?" a fellow soldier inquired one day.

"Talking to Jenny."

"G'wan. There ain't no women aboard. What are you really doin'?"

"Talking to Jenny." Keith flashed the mirror again.

The soldier shook his head and commented, "First time I ever saw a man get shell-shocked before he got off the ship." Keith just grinned but the exchange boosted his morale a bit.

Jenny received the hastily written letter a few days after Keith shipped out. Disappointment filled her. She had hoped so much for a little extra time together. Yet life in wartime left little room for personal problems. Along with the other women, Jenny knitted wool socks and a sweater for her soldier. Once she knew where to send them, they would go to Keith. Every stitch carried her love and prayers. Reduced logging crews continued to harvest timber. Schoolchildren were taught to crochet washcloths for the soldiers. Everyone scrimped and saved to buy savings stamps and Liberty bonds. News came from battles at Belleau-Wood, Chateau Thierry, and Argonne Forest. War songs filled the air: "Over There," "Keep the Home Fires Burning," "Johnny, Get Your Gun."

The most exciting news to reach Three Rivers was that a company of soldiers would arrive soon. Jenny sought out Daddy O'Toone for information.

"Our country needs spruce to build aeroplanes," he told her. "We have an abundance of spruce here. The Spruce Division, as they're called, will harvest it."

Alvin Thomas was assigned to the Spruce Division because of his expertise in woodswork. Trim in his uniform, he assumed the role of big brother to Jenny and cheered her in his off-duty time. One evening when she sat looking east, thinking of the thousands of miles that lay between her and Keith, Alvin quietly said, "I wish it had been me, Jenny."

She felt sick. After all this time, with her engagement announced, surely Alvin wouldn't again tell her he loved her! She recoiled from the thought.

"I don't mean what you think," he quickly said. "I just wish I'd been the one sent overseas and that Keith had been assigned to the Spruce Division."

"Oh, Alvin." She fought a torrent of tears with all her self-control. "You are a good man."

He grinned and put his cap on at a cocky angle. "You aren't the only one who thinks so. Do you know that new little schoolteacher?"

Gladness burst like a firecracker inside her as she pictured the new teacher who had come to finish the year for the former schoolmaster who had entered the army. Jenny teased, "Of course you don't think she's sweet and pretty and nice!"

Alvin's honest eyes shadowed. "Jenny, I'll never speak of it again but I have to tell you no woman will ever take your place. I know now you were right. My love for you was a boyish love. I'm a man now. When this horrible war ends I'm going to marry the teacher if she'll have me. I believe God gave you the wisdom and courage to know the truth." Before she could reply, he lazily stood. "You'll take care of her if I get sent across the pond, won't you?"

"With all my heart." As Jenny watched him march away and heard his whistle, she whispered a prayer of gratitude. All these years he had been such a wonderful friend. Now, if God permitted, their friendship could continue unmarred by regrets.

The coming of the Spruce Division brought other changes to Three Rivers. A few of the soldiers were inclined to malign Jake Lieberman but Alvin put a stop to that. "He's the most patriotic man in town," he told the offenders. "Keep it under your hats, but if it weren't for Jake, our Liberty bond drives would never meet the quota we set."

One Sunday morning in choir Jenny noticed Little Star staring at a khaki-clad soldier sitting with several comrades. She followed her friend's gaze to a lean young man with a swarthy complexion whose coal-black eyes were turned reverently toward the minister. "Who is he?" she whispered when the next hymn was announced and the pianist began an introduction.

"His name's Joe Talbot," she whispered back as the congregation began to sing.

Jenny's eyes opened wider. Although Little Star had always been popular, she hadn't seemed to care about any special boy or young man. Now a warm flush rose under her dusky skin, especially when the handsome soldier glanced at them and smiled. The minute church ended Jenny herded Little Star off to one side. "Tell, tell," she demanded, using their childhood way of asking for secret information.

"He came to the hospital with an axe cut," she related. "I helped Doc Blanchard when he sewed it up. Joe —"

"Joe!" Jenny's eyes sparkled with mischief. "Don't you mean Private Talbot?"

"Do you want to hear what happened or not?" Little Star put her hands on her hips. Jenny learned how the young soldier hung around after being patched up, telling Little Star how much he liked Three Rivers.

"Hmmm. I know what he likes most," she whispered as the subject of discussion determinedly approached them.

"This is Private Joe Talbot," Little Star said. "I'd like you to meet my best friend, Jennifer Ashley."

Jenny liked his cleancut face and the respectful way he ducked his head when he said, "A pleasure, Miss Ashley." Yet she suppressed a laugh at how quickly he turned to Little Star and added, "May I walk home with you?"

A pang went through her when Little Star took the arm he offered and walked away with a smiling backward glance. How many times she and Keith had walked that way! Would they ever again? Suddenly the dark clouds of war invaded her heart as she whispered a prayer for her husband-to-be and the thousands of innocent men, women, and children caught in the bloody maelstrom of World War I. Depression settled over her spirit and she longed for the solitude of Flower Dome. Yet even that left her heart aching as she considered the isolation of the crows'-nest. "Dear God," she whispered. "You know I trust You to help me in all things. Please, if it be Your will, find a way for me to reach Keith. Please, if it be Your will, find a way for me to get Keith's letters."

Two weeks after she reached her crows'-nest Matt Davis arrived for a visit. "I'm supposed to make a personal inspection of the crows'-nests from time to time. Besides, I thought you might like this." He handed her a fat letter post-marked Paris. "Uh, I'll be here a couple of hours. Take your time and write a few letters. I'll take them with me."

"Thank you," she replied. But as soon as he went about his inspection, she looked toward the blue sky and breathed, "And thank You."

In haste she read Keith's letter, promising

to reread it more carefully later. Now she couldn't wait to spill words on paper. She tried to capture the beauty of her surroundings, and not to dwell on her loneliness. He needed to hear cheerful news, not complaints.

"Any overseas letters that come to you will be brought by one of my boys," Matt said just before he left. Jenny could only shake his hand wordlessly, grateful for his concern.

A month passed before Keith's next letter came with the news his outfit was to move out, destination unknown. "Don't worry," he wrote. "Even if you don't know where I am or even if I'm not too sure, God knows. He will take care of me."

Jenny treasured the words and read her few letters until the pages went ragged.

Winter in Three Rivers was no longer the jovial season of years past. Who had the desire to ice skate or coast or sleighride when hometown men fought for their lives on foreign soil? The war became the only topic of conversation between friends and neighbors.

When Jenny rode to town twice a week for mail and groceries, she always stopped to see Uncle Ben and Aunt Carrie, who valiantly kept going in spite of the empty place in their home and hearts. The young woman secretly wished she could be as calm and accepting of life as the Shipleys. Nonetheless, she refrained from telling them how afraid she was for Keith and Donald.

Jake Lieberman always asked about them and it hurt Jenny to tell him she hadn't heard from either man in months. "They are busy, I know, and will write when they can," she told the storekeeper in an effort to convince herself as well as him.

Determined not to let her worries consume her, Jenny pitched in that winter and finished her book. She carefully wrapped it, included return postage, and sent it to a large publishing house on the East Coast. Six weeks later she received a thin letter from the publisher. Her heart leaped. They hadn't returned her manuscript! This must be an acceptance. Yet it didn't look thick enough to contain a contract. She didn't open the letter until she got away from town.

Dear Miss Ashley,

While there is much to admire in your novel Lady of the Lookout, *we regret to inform you it doesn't meet our present needs. We are returning the manuscript*

189

*under separate cover. Please consider us
for other projects in the future.*

The closing was blurred. All the hours, weeks, and months of work she had put into her book were wasted. "Don't be ridiculous," she told herself out loud. "Didn't teachers tell you writers seldom sell their books on the first try? As soon as the manuscript comes back, I'll send it out again."

The second publisher held the manuscript three months before returning it. Without a remonstrative word, Jenny raised her pretty chin and sent it out again. It came back boomerang-fast, so fast Jenny confided to Little Star, "I'm not sure the stamps I licked even had time to dry!"

"You aren't giving up, are you?" Her friend had heard parts of the book and considered it wonderful.

"Not I. I don't have Scottish determination and Irish stubbornness in my blood for nothing." Jenny scratched off the third publisher and promptly mailed the manuscript to the fourth name on her list.

A week later a thin letter came. Jenny eyed it distastefully. Maybe God didn't want her to write after all, yet her book was a testimony of her faith and showed indisputably that Jesus Christ offers the only way to true happiness. "You open it," she told Little Star while both were at the General Store.

Her friend sympathetically slit the envelope and scanned the single page. She let out a whoop that made Jenny jump out of her skin. "Jenny, they like it. They want it. They're sending you a contract!" She held out the letter. *"And they want you to write more."*

The news electrified Three Rivers. Never before had a resident written a story about their own county, about them. For a time, even the war took second place in local gossip.

An ecstatic Jenny decided to serve again on Flower Dome where she planned to write a sequel to her book. Writing was good therapy to ward off her wartime worries, she told herself, as she refused to allow doubt to have a place in her heart. Once it entered, it took all her strength to fight it.

The summer of 1918 passed, Jenny's fifth in a crows'-nest. A few days after she came home, she received an ominous message from the War Department. Corporal Keith Burgess was officially listed as missing in action. Jenny forced herself to read on, then let the letter fall to the floor.

"This doesn't mean he is dead. He may

have been taken prisoner and is being held by the enemy," she said to her parents as she fled their log home.

Longing to be alone, Jenny mounted White Knight and let the gallant horse run. Blood surged through her veins as the wind whipped her hair. So it had come, the news families and sweethearts feared and dreaded. Missing in action. Neither dead nor alive to the world they had known.

"Help me, God, help me," she cried as she urged on White Knight, faster and faster. At last she halted him near a small brook. She slid from the saddle, dropped the reins so he would stand, and lay down on the needle-covered ground. A whisper from the past, a sentence from his letter, crept into Jenny's mind like a cool hand on a warm brow.

Even if you don't know where I am or even if I'm not too sure, God knows.

Then the final triumphant words, *He will take care of me.*

"I know You will, God," she whispered. "Keith accepted Your Son into his heart years before. If anything happens to him, he is still Yours." She lay silent for a long while then brokenly added, "It's just that I don't know what Your will is and oh, I want him to come home so much."

Exhausted, she slept, lulled by singing trees that gently dropped yellow leaves on her tired body. She awakened to a caroling bird perched on a nearby limb. "I feel better," she told White Knight. "I dreamed about Keith and I believe he will come back to me. If he doesn't, I'll still be with him someday."

Three Rivers mourned with her. Most residents couldn't understand how Jenny could smile and answer their sympathetic expressions by saying, "He's coming home." Yet day after day passed without word from either Keith or Donald. Esther Ashley's hair had turned snow white. Deep lines were etched into her husband's face. Ben and Carrie Shipley waited as anxiously for the boy who would have been their son-in-law, and the boy who would be like a son to them someday.

"The worst thing in the world is the waiting," Jenny told Little Star one October evening.

"I know. Rumors keep flying that the war will end soon." She looked at her fingers. "I wish it would. The only good thing to come from it is Joe." Her voice dropped to a whisper. "Jenny, do you regret not marrying Keith before he left?"

Jenny looked at the darkening evening

sky. "I've asked myself that a hundred times," she said.

"And?" A curious intentness held Little Star still.

"I don't know." Jenny turned toward her friend. "We did what we felt was right and yet — if he shouldn't come back —" She dropped her face into her hands. "Perhaps if we had married I would have his son or daughter." She straightened her spine as she did so often in these terrible days. "I guess you just have to decide at each of life's crossroads the way God wants you to go. It doesn't do any good looking back and wondering if you made the right choice." She brushed away her tears. "What about you and Joe?"

"He has asked me to marry him but he's like Keith. He says he won't leave a wife behind. Jenny, it's so true what they say, that men and boys march away to fight, girls and women are left behind to wait and watch."

"And pray."

"And pray." With their hands joined as one, they whispered their prayers of love and desperation in the twilight.

Twelve

Months of wartime gloom were almost erased the day Jenny opened a certain rectangular package from her publisher. As she held her finished book, *Lady of the Lookout*, in her hands for the first time, she marveled at the cover. The illustrator had evidently studied the story and the colorful dust jacket faithfully reproduced characters and events, unlike many books Jenny read.

"I still can't believe it," she told her parents, who eagerly looked over her shoulder. "I never realized how humbling it is to know hundreds, maybe thousands of people will read something I've written." She fingered the words *Jennifer Ashley*.

"You have a God-given talent, Jenny," her wise father said. Andrew's lined face broke into a gentle smile. "It's also a great responsibility. Young girls who read what you write may pattern their choices and actions on what your heroine does. Persons who don't go to church will not only enjoy the story but be exposed to your message of God's love."

"I know." She looked soberly at him and then at her mother, whose still-young looking face contrasted sharply with her waving white hair. "I can never be grateful enough that God has allowed me to do this. If I can touch one heart for Him, all the long hours and hard work will be repaid a thousand times over."

"Remember Emily Dickinson's beautiful poem that expresses that same feeling?" Esther asked. "She said if she could do but one thing to help another, even a fainting robin, her life would not be lived in vain. As followers of the Master we are called to serve. The good you can do in this sad and sinful world will live long after you are gone, Jenny, through your books. Many will remember and thank God for the beauty you offer through using your talent as God would have you do."

"I know. That's why the sequel has been even harder to write than the first book." She sighed, but a deep contentment shone in her brown eyes. "I want every book to be a little better than the one before and I think this one is."

"Then it's finished?" Her mother's eyes filled with eagerness.

Jenny jumped up, spun around, and clasped her precious novel close to her body. "Yes! I'm going to ride White Knight into town this afternoon and send off *Mountain High, Valley Low*." She giggled and the welcome sound rang through the room. "Now *I* have an editor waiting for my book, rather than my book waiting for an editor!"

"I don't suppose you'll be taking this advance copy to town with you," her father teased. "Little Star and Doc and Jake and a few hundred others wouldn't be just waiting to see it, would they?"

Jenny suddenly stopped her mad twirling and caught her breath. "Jake said he plans to stock it in his store. He got the bright idea of having folks sign up if they wanted to buy a copy." Awe crept into her face. "Do you know that more than *one hundred* have signed up? I hope they like it, but it will take a few weeks for the copies to arrive."

"I wouldn't worry about it, dear." Esther smiled proudly.

But the day huge boxes of *Lady of the Lookout* came to Three Rivers, its inhabitants kept the brand-new author busy signing autographs. "Have you read Jenny's book?" became a standard greeting. "It's swell." Matt Davis added the highest praise when he admitted, "I'd like the book even if a flatland furriner had written it!"

One day while riding to town Jenny met Bill Brice's father, Will, driving a team and wagon in for supplies. She noticed how he, too, had aged. Bill had been in some of the worst fighting but was home now after being badly wounded. Not ones to boast, the Brices didn't advertise that their son had won the Badge of Military Merit.* Jenny knew of Bill's award because Little Star had seen the purple badge when she and Doc Blanchard paid a house call at the Brices.

"Miss Ashley." Will Brice courteously removed his hat. "May I have a word with you?"

"Of course." She smiled with genuine fondness at the man whose home had offered hospitality on so many happy occasions before the world turned dark with war.

"I'm thankful to meet you like this. My son Bill would like you to come see him. If we hadn't met on the road, I planned to leave a message at the post office."

"Why, I'd be glad to come," Jenny replied. "I don't really have to go into town

---

*The Badge of Military Merit, which became known as the Purple Heart in 1932, is awarded to members of the armed forces who are wounded in battle. The decoration was established in 1782.

today. I'll just ride back and tell Mother I've changed my plans, then I'll go on to your ranch."

"Thank you. You'll take dinner with them, of course."

"No one who knows Mrs. Brice's cooking would turn down that kind of invitation," she told him. "If I don't see you before I have to leave for home, it's been nice chatting."

"You'll do Bill a world a good," Will told her. "He hates having to stay inside but Doc says it's going to take time for him to heal. If Bill wants to walk straight, he'd better rest that leg." He smiled and chuckled to his horses.

Jenny watched him ride out of sight then galloped home and on to the Brice ranch. She found Bill stretched out on a handmade couch, staring into the dancing flames in the fireplace. He brightened immediately but Jenny wondered what somber images he saw in the fire. She'd already learned from some of the boys who came home how little they wished to talk about the horrors of combat.

"Miss Ashley, how good of you to come!" He made a convulsive motion to rise in her presence, but Jenny lightly pressed his shoulder and shook her head.

"Don't get up. I'll just slip out of my coat and sit here in the chair across from you. Mrs. Brice, it's good to see you."

The hospitable woman in the covering white apron beamed. "Pa said he'd leave a message for you but we didn't expect you so soon."

"We met on the way to town." Jenny handed over her coat, damp from the early November mist, and warmed her hands at the fire. She smiled at two little girls playing dolls nearby who were quickly herded into the kitchen by their mother with the comment they'd just run along and get the dinner going while Bill talked with their visitor.

"You're probably wondering why I asked you to come." A poignant blue light shone from Bill's eyes. "I wanted to send a message the minute I got home, but this old leg kept me pretty sick for a while. It's better now." He patted it. "Doc says in time it will be good as new." His face darkened. "A man feels like a slacker, being home and all, while his buddies are still over there fighting." Desolation in his voice told Jenny more than he ever would.

"Can it really last much longer?" she asked.

"I don't see how." Bill glanced back at the

roaring fire and roused himself with an obvious effort. "Reason I wanted you to come since Doc won't let me do any going is that I ran across Keith Burgess in France."

"You did?" Jenny felt as if someone had knocked the wind from her. She clutched the wooden arms of the rocker and stared at him. "When? I haven't heard from him for months and months." Her voice broke.

"I can't give you a date, but sometime last summer." Bill rubbed his chin with his hand. In the firelight the boyishness that had once been part of his charm had been replaced with a new maturity, a manly look. "Our outfits wound up next to each other and we had a couple of visits. Too busy most of the time." He grimaced and Jenny shuddered at the meaning of the words.

"The last time I saw him was just after I got hit. Our outfits were all mixed up doing what we had to. The firing ceased for some reason and Keith found out I'd been wounded. He got to me just as my buddies were getting me loaded to send to the field hospital."

"How did he look? What did he say?" News after all this time threatened to unnerve Jenny and shatter her splendid control.

"Not much." Bill took a long breath. "I

told him it looked like I'd be going home. He gripped my hand and said, 'Tell Jenny I'm going as soon as I can.' I promised. The firing began again and he raced off toward his outfit, cramming his helmet down over that curly blond hair. But as he glanced back and lifted one hand in the victory signal, his eyes looked bluer than Goat Lake."

She fought tears, as she had done for so many long months. "Bill, you know he's missing in action."

"A lot of men are and turn up eventually," the wounded soldier told her. "I wouldn't get all upset if I were you." Heedless of his leg, he worked to a sitting position and earnestly leaned toward her. "Miss Ashley, that sweetheart of yours isn't a boy who doesn't know how to handle himself. He's a *man*. That time the storm trapped us, did Burgess whimper? You bet your boots he didn't. He stayed with Ed and bucked up his spirits all the time I fought the river." Truth rang in his steady voice. "If any man I know can get through tough going, it's Keith Burgess and I'd stake my life on his courage and daring."

Jenny wordlessly caught both of his hands in hers. "You'll never know what this means to me."

"Oh, I think I do." A little smile softened

the planes of his face. "I saw the look on his face when he said the word Jenny." He hesitated. "Even if he doesn't make it, he's ready. Keith shared his faith with a lot of soldiers scared of dying."

Jenny felt as if the imaginary bands around her chest had at last relaxed. She hadn't been able to pour out her feelings to her parents or to Little Star. Now she tremblingly told Bill, "You do understand. Thank you so much."

He squeezed her hands heartily and advised, "Just keep on praying and hoping. That's what I'm doing." His mask of nonchalance again hid the deep yearnings of his heart to be slogging along with his buddies in the mud of France. Jenny was quieter than usual throughout the excellent dinner. Bill's words to keep on praying and hoping, which undoubtedly had been echoed to countless Allied families around the world, sustained her on the ride home.

November 11, 1918, began the same as usual in Three Rivers, with folks going about their work wearing forced smiles and toting heavy hearts. More of the wounded, some gassed, others shell-shocked, had been arriving on the Galloping Goose. Reunited families tried to hide their shock at the sight of emaciated soldiers whose broad grins showed unbeaten spirits in spite of frail bodies.

Doc Blanchard and Little Star had their hands full as Spanish influenza had also crept into Three Rivers. "It's terrible stuff," Doc told his nurse. "It isn't selective either. Strong men succumb, while others less fit get well. I'm afraid we're going to have a long and tough fight on our hands. One good thing though. Camp Lewis is so filled with sickness they aren't taking any more men."

Into the subdued town the telegraph operator ran, screaming at the top of his lungs, *"It's over! Praise Almighty God, the war is over!"* Up and down Main Street he ran, shouting again and again, *"It's over!"* while a curtain of tears threatened to impede his mission. He nearly fell once, only to regain his balance and go on.

Like a fox streaking for cover, the news ran from family to family, mill to mill, camp to camp. Church bells rang. Mill whistles screeched. Whistle punks went wild, pulling the wires that made donkey whistles blow a continuous blast of praise. Bulls of the woods ordered the men out and crummies jammed with happy loggers headed toward town. That evening every man, woman, and child who could walk, limp, or be carried joined in an impromptu parade down Main Street. Each carried a washtub or tin can, whatever they could get their hands on to make noise. Jake Lieberman danced in the streets, joined by hundreds of others. Never in the history of Three Rivers had there been such a celebration! Little children were told again and again, "The war is over. Thank God for His goodness." Daddy O'Toone was prevailed on to give thanks. No one there would ever forget his streaming eyes, white hair, and beard as he raised his hands like a prophet of old and prayed in a mighty voice that rang through the streets.

Caught up in the frenzy, Jenny refused to spoil the rejoicing by letting her thoughts dwell on Keith and Donald. Surely they would come home soon, along with many others missing from Three Rivers. She clutched Little Star, whose face reflected the glow of bonfires and love. Big Bear's broad face showed how deeply he felt. His tribesmen would also come home, the Great Spirit willing.

In a few short days, however, the town reverted back to its former quiet. Army vehicles and marching soldiers no longer filled the streets. Flags still hung in windows but the outer signs of war had gone.

During the next few months the home boys returned, one by one. Yet neither Donald Ashley nor Keith Burgess was among the returning home guard. The unspoken worry that they and others lay in unmarked graves in foreign soil was shouldered every day by loved ones.

Then in February a white-faced soldier stepped down from the rear platform of the Galloping Goose. Tired from a long, hard journey, he limped down Main Street and into the General Store. "Howdy, Jake."

The big storekeeper turned from a customer. He leaped toward the soldier. "Donald Ashley! Thank God!" Don sank to an upturned nail keg, breathing heavily. "You all right, son?"

"Sure." Don glanced around the store as if eager to determine nothing had changed in his absence. "Have to take it easy for a while. Say, Jake, can you get me a horse from the livery stable?" He grinned and looked more like Jenny than ever. "I'll watch your store."

Jake hurried out but he came back driving a horse-drawn buggy. "This will be easier. Want me to drive you out?" Before Don could say no, Jake blandly added, "That way I can return the rig instead of your folks having to bring it back."

"What about the store?"

A kind-hearted woman who stood waiting to be served quickly volunteered. "*I'll* watch the store. Get along with you!" She brandished a nearby umbrella and shooed the two laughing men out.

"Have things changed much?" Don wanted to know once they settled into the buggy and started out of town.

"Not on the outside. Scars are healing." Jake stared straight between the horse's ears. "Nothing can ever be just like it was," he added when they passed the cemetery with its new white crosses.

A spasm of pain crossed the young soldier's face. "No."

Jake silently regretted his words. Don hadn't been home since Laura Shipley died. "Jenny and your folks will be glad. They must not know you're coming or they'd have been at the depot."

A look of boyhood mischief crept into Don's thin face. "I always did like to surprise them. They're all right, aren't they?"

"Fine," the husky storekeeper said heartily and urged the horse into a faster pace. "Your pa looks older and your ma's hair's gone white but that's from worry."

"And Jenny?" Don shifted on the seat.

"Prettier than ever and just as sweet. Say,

I'll bet you ain't even seen her book yet. It's a good one, talk of the town. Folks keep pestering me, wanting to know when the sequel's coming out." He chuckled. "We're mighty proud of that sister of yours, and you."

Don waved off the praise with a shake of his head. As the buggy jostled down the country road, he quietly observed the faint green signs of spring that hovered almost breathlessly for the warm days ahead. When they reached the Ashley ranch, he said, "Jake, you don't mind if I go in alone, do you?"

"Of course not, Donald. I have to get this horse and buggy back. Besides, I need to see if my new help has put everything on sale and run me out of business!" The understanding man turned the buggy around and headed toward town as soon as Don reached the porch.

Now that the moment he'd waited for so long had arrived, Don found it hard to turn the knob and step inside. It felt like centuries had passed since he gaily went out the door. Yet the moment he walked in and called, "Father, Mother, I'm home! Jenny, where are you?" the hands of the clock seemed to turn backward as if all the time in between had simply been a nightmare.

"Donald, my son. Oh, thanks be to God!"
White-haired Esther reached him first,
glory in her face that blurred before him,
arms around her man-child. She released
him only when her husband strode to them.
Flying feet announced Jenny's arrival and
she slipped under Andrew's arm to her
brother.

"Oh, Don, we've waited so long." She
laughed and cried at the same time.

As Donald gripped the chairback for support, his family quickly escorted him to a
settee by the fire. "I just don't have my
strength back yet," he murmured in appreciation.

"Bring hot coffee, Jenny." Andrew Ashley
peeled off Don's coat. "Have you had
dinner?"

"Nothing worth mentioning. Mother,
could you make hot biscuits? I've dreamed
about them so many nights on our ship and
when I lay in the hospital. Our ship was tor-
pedoed and sank but most of us drifted until
we were finally picked up." He broke off his
dialogue suddenly and Jenny suspected it
was all they would hear of his experiences.

By the time Esther took golden brown biscuits out of the oven and dished up Tarheel
(cream-style) gravy and hot applesauce,
Don lay sound asleep on the couch. They

roused and fed him; he slept again. "Didn't get a lot of rest in the hospital," he apologized.

Not until the first week of March did he rouse himself from his lethargy, although each day brought more sparkle to his eyes. One day when he and Jenny were alone after breakfast he said in a low voice, "Will you go to the cemetery with me?"

"Of course." Her heart ached. Yet the visit proved to be good for both of them. They sat in the grass next to Laura's grave and spoke quietly of her shining example during her short life. Don confessed, "Many times when I faced danger I thought of her and how she'd want me to go on. I remembered her unshakable faith in God and that has deepened my own feelings for Him." He plucked a blade of grass and chewed on it. "Jenny, do you think she'd mind if someday, a long time from now, I married someone else?"

Jenny carefully considered his question, knowing what she said could make a difference. She had loved Laura, too, and in many ways knew her better than Don. "I think Laura would be sad for you to spend your life alone," she said softly. "Don, if you meet a Christian woman you can love, God will let you know if it is right."

"Thanks, little sister." In their shared silence Jenny heard the glorious birdsongs from nearby cedars, a paean to the sun-dappled spring day. "You've never heard anything more about Keith?"

"Just what I told you Bill Brice said."

"Don't give up hope," he told her. "If he were taken prisoner he may still come home. I hope so." He stood and brushed grass from his pants. "Jenny, I'm going to reenlist in the merchant marine and make it a career. It would be just too hard to stay in Three Rivers without Laura." His words came out rapidly. "Do you think Father and Mother will understand?"

"Of course." She slipped her hand into her brother's and tugged until he stood beside her, tall and strong once more.

"I won't go back for several weeks," he promised.

Jenny squelched an involuntary sigh and laughed. "Good. With all the weddings, you wouldn't want to miss being here."

His eyes darkened but he smiled. "Who would have thought Alvin or Little Star would be married before either of us? Life's plumb pecooliar, as Big Jim Callihan said when he found a lizard in the toe of his boot one morning."

Jenny laughed. How good to have Don

home. She must treasure every moment.

Yet when first Alvin and his schoolteacher bride, and then Little Star and Joe stood before Daddy O'Toone and pledged their love, Jenny had to bite her lip to keep from crying. The war had ended in November. If Keith were coming home, why hadn't he reached Three Rivers by now? In the anticipation of his coming, she had reluctantly told Matt Davis she wouldn't work at Power Dome this year. Now she wished she had kept the job.

"My sister, I wish you the great happiness I have found," Little Star whispered after her simple wedding. Jenny strongly suspected she had refused a large church ceremony because of Laura and Keith's absence. She and Joe merely went to Daddy O'Toone's home with only Big Bear, Jenny, Don, and Doc Blanchard present. Little Star took her wedding vows wearing a charming white dress but changed into buckskins for her wedding trip.

"To Glacier Peak," she confided. "Joe will love it."

As Jenny hugged the new Mrs. Joe Talbot, she felt one more precious childhood tie being put asunder.

Thirteen

As the lull of peacetime fell over Three Rivers, Jenny felt an inevitable letdown. Through all the war years, through the Armistice, and the influenza epidemic that followed, she had forced herself to keep going and to serve. When life grew unbearable, she turned to her writing. No matter how insufferable her world might be, she knew she would find respite in putting words to the page.

Lady of the Lookout had not proved to be a bestseller, although sales and critical reviews had deemed the book a success. Jenny felt especially proud of her efforts when she received the following letter from a teenage girl.

> *Dear Miss Ashley,*
> *I have just finished reading your book. You will never know how much it means to me, or how I feel God had you write it because I needed it. I've been a*

*Christian for a long time but I doubted
Him when my brother didn't come home
from the war. How could God let him be
killed?*

*When I read how your heroine trusted
God in all her troubles, I realized I had
to find Him again and let Him heal me.*

*Miss Ashley, please write more books.
I have wanted to write since I was a
little girl. Now if God will forgive me
and help me, maybe someday I too can
write for Him.*

Jenny cried over the letter. She could
barely fathom that she had been allowed to
touch this life with her writing and she responded immediately.

Dear Ruth,

*Persons like you make my life rich
and sweet. I am humbled to know my
story helped you become closer to God.
Do you know that your name from the
Hebrew means "friend of beauty?" I
sense in your letter a longing for higher
things than are found in this world. I
know God has already forgiven your
doubts.*

*I'll tell you a true story. Years ago I
used to read my favorite authors and*

wish that I could grow up and write like them. Now here we are and you are saying the same thing.

If God can use those particular talents, you will find out by working hard and always acknowledging Him as your Source. God bless, my new friend. By the way, the sequel to Lady of the Lookout, Mountain High, Valley Low, *is due to be issued any time.*

Keep trusting our Master. It's the only happy way to live.

As Jenny signed the letter her gaze drifted back to the closing sentence. How much easier to write the words than to live day after lonely day with the dark clouds of uncertainty hovering over her! Yet deep in her heart she wanted to believe Keith would return to her, even after months of silence.

One mid-June afternoon Jenny lay in the shade of the maple tree that spread its leaves above Pixie House. Never had she felt more alone, not at boarding school or even in the crows'-nest. Suddenly she cried out to God. "They're all gone. Laura. Keith. Don. Little Star. Oh, dear God, I am so lonely!" Tammy whined and snuggled closer. Did the faithful dog sense her owner's distress? White Knight lifted his head from munching grass and whinnied.

Unable to bear the crushing weight of too many months of worry, Jenny lay still and listened. The hum of bees, the songs of a dozen birds, the distant "ch-chunk" of a frog were all familiar and reassuring. The cry of an eagle, however, brought her to a sitting position. Eagles held a certain fascination for Jenny. Proud and strong, they scorned earth and built their nests on the tallest peaks.

A favorite Scripture came to mind. How many times Mother had read Matthew 10, verses 29 and 31, to Don! "Are not two sparrows sold for a farthing? and one of them shall not fall on the ground without your Father then Fear ye not therefore, ye are of more value than many sparrows."

Jenny watched the eagle until it sailed out of sight. "Dear God, You promised many times not to forsake those who love and serve You," she murmured in a voice barely above the sigh of the maple leaves fluttering above her. "No matter how many friends and loved ones leave me, You never will." Comforted, she rose and walked slowly home, followed by her faithful dog and horse.

The week before the Fourth of July proved bittersweet. Jenny summoned all her newfound strength to ride to town and see the elaborate decorations being foisted once again. So many memories crowded Three Rivers and Independence Day! She counted them off in her mind.

Six years ago she stepped off the Galloping Goose without a regret that her schooldays had ended. Six years ago she raced White Knight and won not only first prize but Keith Burgess's admiration as well. Six years ago she worked as a flunky. She smiled at the memory of the child she had been and laughed at how bashful she was when she met Keith at the logging camp.

Five years ago she sent her first mirror signals from Flower Dome to Pinnacle Peak.

Two years ago the war began, she continued her lookout duties, and life became a mix of contradictions, fire and flood, joy and sorrow, life and death.

What would the last half of 1919 bring? Another book contract? More opportunities to witness of her Lord through her writing?

"Jenny, we're back." A caroling voice interrupted her reverie.

"Little Star! You look wonderful." Jenny hugged her friend and a great gladness rolled over her. "I thought you'd be gone at least another few days."

The Indian bride cast a roguish glance at her smiling husband. "Joe and I wouldn't miss this Fourth of July celebration for anything. It's bound to be the best ever, what with the war being over." Quick compassion sprang to her dark eyes. "Jenny, have you heard anything more about Keith?"

"No."

Joe Talbot unobtrusively moved to one side and his new wife asked, "Would you rather not discuss it?" She glanced up and down Main Street, bright with flags and bunting, so much the same and yet changed forever.

Jenny shook her head. "There's really nothing to say but I'm glad you asked. Most folks never mention him to me." A lump came to her throat. "That's worse than speaking of him."

"He may still return." Little Star put her arm around her friend. "Joe says it wouldn't surprise him, even though all he knows of Keith is what I've told him."

"I'm glad you're back," Jenny whispered. "It's been lonely, especially since Don left. Tell me, where are you going to live?"

Little Star's eyes glistened. "Halfway between Three Rivers and your home! Joe saved most of his military pay and I always hoarded my nursing money. And Jenny,

Doc Blanchard says he will be tickled to death to have me work for him, at least until little ones come along." A lovely light shone in her eyes and made her more beautiful.

"That's wonderful. Now I will have a good place to stop when I ride into town," Jenny rejoiced. With Little Star's return and news, the world didn't seem as empty.

"Are you doing anything in the program this year?"

"I've been asked to sing 'The Star-Spangled Banner,' " Jenny said.

"No one can do it better. Sure wish I'd been blessed with talents like some folks I know," Little Star teased. "Such as singing and writing and —"

"Don't be silly, you have a lovely voice! Besides, you're what Doc calls a crackerjack nurse and I'll bet you'll be the best wife and mother in the county," Jenny retorted in a loud voice.

Joe Talbot came back over and embraced his wife. "She's already the best wife." He patted his stomach. "I'm in danger of getting fat from her camp cooking. Can't imagine what it will be like once we get settled and she has an actual stove!"

Jenny escaped in their shared laughter. Someday, when she accepted the fact that Keith would not be back, might God send another fine man into her life? She rebelled at the idea, yet she knew God's ways were not always her ways. For now, she must live one day at a time. The words of Percy Bysshe Shelley's "Ode to the West Wind" came to her: *If Winter comes, can Spring be far behind?*

The night before the Fourth of July, Esther Ashley put the final stitches in a pink lace gown for her daughter. "It turned out well," she admitted with modest pride. "You know, although this dress is lace, the one you wore the year you won the horse race was very similar. You haven't changed a lot on the outside." Jenny winced when she realized how keenly aware those who loved her had been of her personal turmoil.

"Sing your heart out, Jenny," Andrew Ashley advised the next morning when he escorted his womenfolk to town and the celebration.

Rather than letting speeches get lost in excitement, this year the town fathers decreed that recognition of Independence Day would come first. A raised platform held the local band, already tootling away and warming up when the Ashleys arrived. Bill Brice, Joe Talbot, Alvin Thomas, and all the others who had served in the military looked uncomfortable but resigned to being back in uniform. Before the festivities began Bill muttered to Jenny, "Soon's the parade's over, we'll get into other clothes. I plan to win this year's race on Dynamite, seeing how as a certain young lady isn't entering!"

She laughed. "I hope you do." Her laughter faded when Doc Blanchard beckoned her to the platform. A hush fell over the crowd. Jenny heard a whisper, "She is so brave. All this time and —"

"Shh, she'll hear you."

The well-intentioned comment went straight to the singer's heart. In a tremulous voice she said four words: "For all our boys." The band played a few lines and then Jenny's voice empowered the timeless lyrics.

> *Oh! say can you see, by the dawn's early light,*
> *What so proudly we hailed at the twilight's last gleaming?*
> *Whose broad stripes and bright stars . . .*

The song went on through the first verse to its glorious conclusion.

> *Oh! say, does that star-spangled banner yet wave*

O'er the land of the free and the home of the brave?

The band went into the second verse. Jenny clutched her throat and faltered. Had she strained her voice on the high note?

Her eyes, though teary with emotion, had seen something that drove all thoughts away. She blinked and looked again. With a low cry she darted from the platform and pushed her way through the mob, straight toward a tall figure standing a little beyond the crowd.

Smiling, he watched her come, a small mirror held tight in his upraised hand.

"Oh, God, thank You!" Jenny repeated again and again as she ran into his two strong arms.

"Burgess."

"It's Keith Burgess!"

"He was missing in action."

The crowd began shouting and cheering. Jake Lieberman wiped unashamed tears away and led the rush toward the pair who stood oblivious to the chaos. "Son, she never lost faith that you'd come back," he said simply.

"That's more than I can say," Keith admitted. His honest blue eyes held shadows. "All that matters is that the war is over and I'm home."

Someone started the old hymn, "Praise God from Whom All Blessings Flow." The celebration seemed sparked with new fire now that the last of the Three Rivers men had returned. Bill Brice shook hands with Keith. He said nothing, but the muscles in his face worked and Jenny knew they shared a bond of suffering that could only have been forged by the war.

When the tension grew too great, Bill said, "This one's for you, Burgess. I rode for you once before. Now Dynamite's going to strut his stuff." Not since the long-ago race Jenny won had there been such an amazing event. Dynamite showed his heels to the other horses in both heats, making them look as if they still had one hoof in the barn. Jenny Ashley stood as if in a daze, her arm entwined around the young soldier's, her eyes focused only on him. For her the long war had truly ended when she looked beyond the crowd and caught the signal of love from Keith's mirror.

Epilogue

A few days later the loyal citizenry of Three Rivers donned their Sunday best and made their way to the little white church with its steeple pointing toward heaven. Once inside, everyone good-naturedly moved close together to make room for others. No one wanted to miss the wedding of Jennifer Ashley and Keith Burgess.

Jenny stood in a small room out of sight, gowned in white and carrying pink roses. No orchids or gardenias for her. She closed her eyes and visualized the altar, decked in green ferns and bouquets of wildflowers the Sunday school children had so eagerly picked. In a short time she and Keith would be husband and wife. Their honeymoon would be postponed for a day or two since Keith had to report in Seattle for his final discharge. When they returned, together they would then head for the mountains, following much the same route she had traveled long ago with Laura, Little

Star, and Big Bear.

"It's time," her father reminded. "Donald took your mother in. I'm glad he could be here."

"So am I," she whispered. With an unspoken prayer she might always be worthy of Keith's love and that their lives would make a difference for God, Jenny placed her hand on Andrew's arm and took the first step into her new life.

Daddy O'Toone delivered the traditional service in great style, but Jenny was aware of little save the famous last words, "I pronounce you husband and wife. Whom God has joined together, let no man put asunder." Keith lifted her veil and bent and kissed her. Then he whispered, "No more crows'-nests for us, my darling. It will be our own nest and wee ones." Jenny blushed and turned to receive all the happy wishes her friends and neighbors had to offer.

The next morning Keith and Jenny climbed aboard the Galloping Goose and waved goodbye to the friends who had come to see them off. When the conductor shouted, "All aboard!" and the wheels began clacking, one solemn little girl who had helped decorate the church sidled close to Little Star and tugged on her gown. "Please, are they going away forever? Won't they come back?" Tears sprang to her troubled eyes.

Little Star knelt and caught her close. "They will be back soon. You see, dear, this is Jenny's town." Her dark eyes glowed with thankfulness and love.